Henry Rush Boss

Sketches of the History of Ogle County, Ill., and the Early Settlement of the Northwest

SALZWASSER VERLAG

Henry Rush Boss

Sketches of the History of Ogle County, Ill., and the Early Settlement of the Northwest

Reprint of the original, first published in 1859.

1st Edition 2023 | ISBN: 978-3-37514-244-5

Verlag (Publisher): Salzwasser Verlag GmbH, Zeilweg 44, 60439 Frankfurt, Deutschland
Vertretungsberechtigt (Authorized to represent): E. Roepke, Zeilweg 44, 60439 Frankfurt, Deutschland
Druck (Print): Books on Demand GmbH, In de Tarpen 42, 22848 Norderstedt, Deutschland

SKETCHES

OF THE

HISTORY OF OGLE COUNTY, ILL.

AND THE

EARLY SETTLEMENT OF THE NORTHWEST

WRITTEN FOR THE POLO ADVERTISER.

POLO, ILLINOIS:
PUBLISHED BY HENRY R. BOSS,
Advertiser Office, Mason Street.

1859.

HISTORY OF OGLE COUNTY,

CHAPTER I.

INTRODUCTORY.

No apology is needed for the publication at this time of a History of Ogle County. There are few who will not at once recognize the importance of the work.

The following sketches, perhaps, can hardly be dignified with the title of a history, from a lack of order and arrangement which is almost unavoidable under the circumstances; but such as they are, we believe them to be accurate and reliable. In looking to books for materials, we have endeavored to find such as could be relied upon for accuracy and impartiality, while the accounts given by the pioneers now living are from men who can be relied upon for probity and integrity and a knowledge of the things whereof they have spoken. We have consulted Hakluyt's Voyages, Hennepin's Works, Burnet's Notes, Bancroft's History of the United States, Hart's History of the Valley of the Mississippi, Shelton's History of Michigan, Ford's History of Illinois, Peck's Western Annals, and many other works, and in some instances have adopted parts of them as best expressing what we wanted to show.

We have commenced with a rapid sketch of the Early Settlement of the Northwest, which is inseparably connected with the history of our own county. In this we have drawn from the most authentic sources such facts as presented themselves to us as possessing interest and were well sustained. The settlement of the entire Valley of the Mississippi, of which this section is a part, is so connected with our own local history, that we could not in justice pass it by.

The Black Hawk War, in which many of our citizens took a part, is a matter in which we have all felt a deep interest, occurring, as it did, where our own firesides are now located. Its history is full of incidents bordering upon the romantic, and far more thrilling than the veriest blood-and-thunder fiction ever published.

We have merely called our work a history for want of a better title. It is necessarily written during a pressure of multitudinous engagements, which prevent our giving these sketches an arrangement and classification which we could readily give were they all written previous to their publication.

CHAPTER II.

On Easter Sunday, in the year 1512, Juan Ponce de Leon, a comrade of Christopher Columbus, discovered the continent of America, near St. Augustine, and named the new country Florida. The causes which led to this discovery were the same which actuated scores of the adventurers of that day, viz: a thirst for gold and a desire to find the fountain, said to exist in the wilds of America, which was thought to have the power of renewing the youth of those who drank of or bathed in its waters. Though unsuccessful in their own search after these objects, the earlier adventurers bore back to their native land marvellous tales of what *might* be found, and thus stimulated others to renew a search in which they had failed. Among the most noted of those whom these reports reached was Ferdinand De Soto, who, in the month of May, 1539, or about three hundred and nineteen years ago, anchored his vessel near the coast of the Peninsula of Florida, in Tampa Bay. He was accompanied by a brilliant band of followers, many of whom were of noble birth, all of them eager to clutch the golden treasures which were said to exist in America. The career of De Soto and his ill-fated band is familiar to all our readers. The ill success of their search after gold, their failure to discover the fountain of youth, the sickness and wasting away of the troop, and the death and burial in the Mississippi of their high-spirited and energetic leader, are "familiar as household words." Of the "gallant six hundred" who accompanied De Soto in his setting-out, about one-half left their bones to bleach on the morasses and mountains of the South from Georgia to Arkansas. This, the first expedition of Europeans into the Valley of the Mississippi, left no trace behind it. They gained nothing for themselves or those to come after them, and the only effect produced was to embitter the minds of the Indians and to dishearten those who might otherwise have attempted to explore this valley.

During the succeeding century not an European made his appearance in the territory now known as "the West." In 1616, Le Caron, a French Franciscan, had penetrated to the streams which run into Lake Huron, and in 1634 two Jesuits had founded the first mission among the rivers and marshes of the region east of that lake; but it was in 1641, just one hundred years after De Soto reached the Mississippi, that the first Canadian envoys met the savage nations of the Northwest at the Falls of St. Mary, below the outlet of Lake Superior.* It was not until 1659

* Western Annals, p. 28 *et seq.*

HISTORY OF OGLE COUNTY. 3

First Missionary Station on Lake Superior—Marquette Embarks for the Mississippi—Dangers foretold—Legend of Piasau.

that even any of the fur-traders spent a winter in the frozen regions about the great lake, nor till 1660 that the unflinching devotion of the missionaries caused the first station to rise upon its borders. The earliest of the lasting habitations of the white man among the Indians of the Northwest was built in 1665 by Father Claude Allouez. After this venerable man came Claude Dablon and James Marquette to St. Mary's Falls and there founded a mission. Nicholas Perrot, agent for Talon, the intendant of Canada, explored Lake Michigan as far as Chicago in 1670. The year following these explorations of Perrot, the French formally took possession of the Great Northwest, in the presence of an assembled multitude of the aborigines, who had come from every part of the surrounding country to witness the ceremony; and in the same year Marquette gathered a little band of listeners at Point St. Ignatius, on the main land north of the island of Mackinac. Unlike the ambitious De Soto, who had found the Father of Waters in his search for the mystic fountain, mighty cities and mines of gold, the heart of the no less ambitious Marquette yearned for the numberless hosts of the children of God, who, he rightly fancied, were living upon its fertile banks, and upon whom the light of the Gospel never shone. Pursuant to the orders of Talon, on the 13th of May, 1673, with Monsieur Joliet, of Quebec, and five boatmen, this noble man left Michilimackinac in two bark canoes, with a small store of Indian corn and jerked meat, bound they knew not whither. The first nation they visited begged them to desist from their daring adventure; they told them of ferocious savages and bloodthirsty warriors upon the "Great River," who would slaughter them with the least provocation; of a demon, who engulfed in the boiling waters around him any who might come within the reach of his fatal power;[*] and should they pass these dangers, there were heats by which they must certainly perish.

"I thanked them," says Marquette, "for their good advice, but I told them that I could not follow it, since the salvation of souls was at stake, for which I should be overjoyed to give my life."

They passed through Green Bay and entered Fox River, and after having cruelly cut their feet upon the stones, while dragging their canoes through the strong rapids, arrived at an Indian village where the Miamis, Mascoutens and Kickapoos lived together in harmony. Here Father Allouez, of whom we have before spoken, had preached, and evidently not without some effect; for, to their surprise, Marquette and his party found in the middle of the town a cross on which had been hung bows and arrows, belts and skins, which "these good people had offered to the Great Manitou, to thank him because

*The reference here is to the legend of Piasau, or the monster bird that devoured men, of which some rude Indian paintings were seen thirty years since on the cliffs above the city of Alton, and the Indians, as they passed in their canoes, made offerings by dropping tobacco and other articles, valuable in their estimation, into the river. John Russell, Esq., of Illinois, wrote this "Indian Tradition" into a beautiful story that went the rounds of periodical literature in 1840.—*Western Annals.*

4   HISTORY OF OGLE COUNTY.

Marquette on the Wisconsin River—At an Indian Feast—He Reaches the Arkansas—Returns to Green Bay—His Death.

he had taken pity on them during the winter, and had given them an abundant chase." Here was the bound of discovery; not even the most daring Frenchman had ever ventured into the wilds beyond. It is not to be wondered at, therefore, that the bravery of those seven men, who were casting themselves upon the mercy of savages, should excite astonishment in the minds of those " braves," who better know the dangers beyond.

Leaving these hospitable strangers, with two guides to lead them through the lakes and marshes which abounded in that region, they started for the Wisconsin river, which, they were told, rose about three leagues distant and fell into the Mississippi. Strengthening their souls with prayer to the Virgin Mother, they committed themselves to the hands of God and the bosom of a westward flowing river. Although the Wisconsin is a sand-barred stream, and hard to navigate, their troubles were compensated by its vine-clad islands, the waving meadows along its banks, the graceful slopes and music ringing forests. After floating down the river for six days, with inexpressible joy they entered the Mississippi. On they floated down the "Great River," with living things above, beneath, on either hand, but nowhere could be seen a vestige of man, until the 21st day of June, when a trail was discovered on the western bank, which, Marquette and Joliet following, led to an Indian village at a short distance from the river. Here they were hospitably received, and they found themselves in a town of the " Illinois." The rest of the company

were immediately brought, and after many ceremonies, a feast was prepared of not exactly modern style, the first course consisting of hominy, the second of fish, the third of dog, and the last of roast buffalo.

Proceeding on their journey, they found the river all along, and on either side, inhabited by these rude children of the forest.

They touched at points now well known to every citizen of our State, till they reached the Arkansas or " Akamsca," as it was called, when they determined to return to the North, being deterred by the dangers which beset the route to the mouth of the Mississippi; and on the 19th of July they commenced to retrace their steps and turned towards the Lake, and reached Green Bay in September without loss or injury.

The circumstances attending the death of the simple-minded Marquette were affecting. In the month of May, in 1675, as he was passing with his boatmen up Lake Michigan, he proposed to land at the mouth of a stream running from the peninsula, and perform mass. Imitating the example of his Master before him, he " went apart to pray." Not returning as soon as they expected, his boatmen, remembering that he had said something about his death being near at hand, went to seek him. In the act of prayer he had fallen asleep forever. In the sands on the shores of the " Great Lakes" this man of boundless sympathy found a narrow home. A river in Michigan bears the name of the missionary, at the mouth of which it is said his body was buried. His remains were removed

HISTORY OF OGLE COUNTY.   9

Robert De La Salle—His Projects—First Vessel Built on the Lakes—Commerce of the Lakes.

a year after, by the Indians, and conveyed to his mission at Mackinac. The place of his death, however, has never yet been definitely ascertained, though several writers agree in fixing it at or near the mouth of the Marquette River.

Among those who had listened to the story of Marquette's expedition to the west, was Robert De La Salle. He was a native of Normandy, and having lost his patrimony from some cause unknown to us, came to the new world to seek his fortune. He had long had in his mind the project of crossing the continent, and thus opening a shorter way to China and the East. Glad was he to receive from Marquette the suggestion, that by following up the Mississippi, or turning into some of the rivers that flow into it from the west, his end could be accomplished without great difficulty. He immediately laid before the Governor of Canada his ambitious design. He proposed, as a first step, to re-build Fort Frontenac, now Kingston, Canada, (which took its name from the Governor,) which proposition he had good reason to expect would meet the wishes of the Governor. Nor were his expectations wrong. Frontenac warmly endorsed his whole plan, for he saw, if La Salle's project was successful, that a chain of forts upon the lakes and rivers which so wonderfully unite the Great West should link the Gulf of Mexico to Canada, the power of France would be unmeasured, and he himself would receive unequaled glory, if, as he hoped, all could be accomplished under his administration. By his advice La Salle at once started for

France. The plans of the penniless adventurer were warmly approved of by the French authorities. La Salle was made a Chevalier, and was invested with the seigniory of Fort Frontenac, provided he should re-build it. He returned to Canada and labored for nearly two years upon the Fort, and then, in the year 1677, went again to France to report progress. In the latter part of September, 1678, he returned to Fort Frontenac vested with new authority, and having gained new privileges.

On the 22d of January, 1676, the docks for building a vessel were made at two leagues above Niagara Falls, and on the 26th of the same month, the keel and some other pieces being ready, La Salle drove the first pin of the first vessel ever built to navigate the Great Lakes of the North and the Northwest. We may be pardoned if we pause here to take a survey of the changes which have been made in less than two centuries. It is with no little pride that we point to the vast commerce whose sails now dot every portion of these Lakes, and which is rivalling the commerce of the ocean. In a recent lecture, Lieut. Maury stated, on the authority of Col. Graham's report to the department at Washington, that the shipping and commerce of Lake Michigan amount to $218,000,000. He also stated that the value of the shipping and commerce passing over the St. Clair Flats averages *daily*, for two hundred and thirty days of each year, $1,129,223. At this estimate, one hundred and twelve vessels, valued with their cargoes $10,000 each, must pass over the Flats daily. He stated the value

6   HISTORY OF OGLE COUNTY.

La Salle's Expedition with Hennepin—His Death—De Soto's Dream of Gold Realized—Early Settlements in Illinois.

of the lake commerce to be $200,000,000 to each lake, except Lake Erie, which is estimated at $300,000,000. What a vast change has been made since the launching of the *Griffin*, two centuries ago!

On the 7th of August, 1779, La Salle with his little company, of whom one was Louis Hennepin, a monk of the Recollet order, started for Illinois. On the 3d of December, they left Fort St. Joseph, which was built at that time by La Salle, who left a garrison of ten men, and built Fort Crevecœuer, on the Illinois River, early in 1680. From Fort Crevecœuer La Salle returned to Canada, while Hennepin continued the exploration. On the last day of February, 1680, he started for the Mississippi, which he reached after a journey of seven days, and by the 11th of April had paddled up the Wisconsin. On the 1st of May he reached St. Anthony's Falls, where he was taken prisoner and remained three months. Hennepin returned to New-France in November of the same year, and published his first work in 1684, in France.

We find La Salle again, in August, 1681, on his way up the Lakes, and on the 3d of November at the St. Joseph's, undismayed at the losses and ill fortune to which he had been subjected. On the 16th of April, 1682, the Chevalier and his party discovered the three passages by which the Mississippi discharges its waters into the Gulf. La Salle here took possession of the country for his king, and erected a column bearing the arms of France and an appropriate inscription.

We are compelled to pass over the "haps and mishaps" with which this lion-hearted adventurer met, and simply record his death by the hands of his own comrades, in 1687.

De Soto's dream of gold is realized. After the lapse of nearly three centuries and a half, we now, in this year of grace 1859, hear more reliable tales than he did, of the discoveries of immense heaps of wealth on the eastern slope of the Rocky Mountains. In the Valley of the Mississippi, where the bones of the adventurous Spaniard were laid, we find all that he sought, save the fountain of youth. Populous cities and stores of countless wealth are on every side of us; while he who so bravely sought what we now see and enjoy, sleeps in the bosom of the Father of Waters, where no monumental stone shall ever rise to mark his last resting-place.

CHAPTER III.

Although La Salle came very far short of a realization of his ambitious dreams, he played no insignificant part in the early settlement of the Northwest. He established several permanent forts, and thus opened the gateway for the tide of immigration, so that as early as 1693 we hear of mission stations among the Illinois which were so permanent as to identify the places of their location, and many of them are now flourishing cities. Kaskaskia, Cahokia and Peoria were prominent points at the above date, although the precise time of their first settlement is not positively known, except it be that of Peoria, which is situated on the site of the old Fort Crevecœur, which La Salle built,

HISTORY OF OGLE COUNTY. 7

D'Iberville's Expedition to the Mississippi—Founds Fort Rosalie—Cadillac founds Fort Pontchartrain in 1701.

as we have said, in the early part of 1680. These, however, must be regarded as mission stations, where a few priests, under the supervision of Father Gravier, who was the first to reduce the language of the Indians to grammatical order, ministered to the spiritual wants of the natives, until the year 1712, when they became known as French settlements. Whatever be the time of the first settlement of the three places named above, it is evident that Kaskaskia comes first in order; very soon after, Cahokia; and next Peoria.

La Salle's project, to discover and settle Louisiana by sea, was next undertaken by D'Iberville in 1697. Like his predecessor, he met favor in the court of France, and with two ships, on the 17th of October, 1698, he left the court of France, and on the 2d of March, 1699, he entered the mouth of the Mississippi having accomplished with little difficulty what had long been regarded as almost an impossibility. After dispatching one of his vessels to France with the news of his success, he began slowly to ascend the vast river; and after gaining a limited acquaintance with its appearance for a short distance above its mouth, he built a fort near the mouth of the Mobile, and leaving a suitable garrison, returned to France. While he was gone, the commander of the fort, being absent on an expedition about the mouth of the Mississippi, met a British vessel carrying twelve cannon. Assuming an imposing authority, he informed his rivals that if they did not leave the river immediately he would bring to bear his forces, which were amply sufficient to oblige them to do so. This had its desired effect, and the Britons left the French in quiet possession for the time being only, for they believed their claim was paramount, and they afterwards supported it with more courage than upon this occasion, and it was settled only at the conclusion of the French war of 1756. D'Iberville returned from France in January, 1700, and having heard of the advances of the British, he formally took possession of the great valley of the West, and built a fort on the bank of the river. He then proceeded up the river and laid the corner stone of Fort Rosalie, where the city of Natchez, Miss., now stands. Leaving a mining company to search for copper, which company was not very successful, he returned to France, but visited this country again on the following year. Excepting a settlement on the Mobile, he effected very little. In the year 1708 he died, having written his name among the successful adventurers of his age. The French government, losing very much of its confidence in these modes of procedure to establish actual settlements, and thinking that a single man, who had his own pecuniary interests at stake, would do more for her advancement, gave the actual possession of Louisiana to Crozat for fifteen years. Meeting with nothing but loss, he surrendered his privilege in 1797, having kept it five years.

In the month of June, 1701, Fort Pontchartrain was founded by Cadillac where the city of Detroit now stands.

The management of affairs in the west now passed into the hands of the noted Mississippi company, or Company of the

West. The government nourished with every possible care this element of ruin, authorizing it to sell its shares for public stock taken at par, which was selling at 60 to 70 per cent. discount, giving exclusive right of the Mississippi country trade for twenty-five years, the monopoly of the Canadian beaver trade and the tobacco trade, the exclusive right of trading in Asia and the East Indies, the farming of the public revenues, the exclusive right of coining for nine years, &c., &c., until in April, 1720, the stock of the Company had risen to 2050 per cent., while it had in circulation notes for $200,000,000. Then the bubble burst. The decline of stocks began in April, and in spite of the government, the company was bankrupt in May. Yet this strange mania was not without some benefits. It introduced the cultivation of tobacco, indigo, rice and silk; it opened the lead mines of Missouri, in the hope of finding silver, and wheat, in the Northern portions of the country, began to assume a place among the commodities of the day, and withal the French settlements were considerably extended. "Law's Mississippi Scheme" is now almost proverbial for the magnitude of its promises and the narrowness of the basis on which it rested.

When the Company of the West gave up Louisiana again to the French government, it was determined to strike terror into the Chickasaws, who constantly interfered with the trade on the Mississippi. On the 10th of May, 1736, D'Artaguette, governor of Illinois, and Vincennes, appeared in the Chickasaw country, leading a small body of French and more than a thousand northern Indians; but they were disappointed in not meeting Bienville, the king's lieutenant, whom they expected. They waited ten days for his appearance, when, fearful of exhausting the patience of his red allies, D'Artaguette ordered an onset. Two Chickasaw stations were successfully carried, but in attacking the third, the French leader fell, when the Illinois fled, leaving D'Artaguette and Vincennes, who would not leave him, in the hands of the Chickasaws. Five days afterwards, Bienville appeared, but it was too late; the Chickasaws were on their guard, and had so fortified their position that the French attacked them in vain. On the 20th of May, D'Artaguette had fallen; on the 27th, Bienville had failed in his assault; on the 31st, throwing his cannon into the river, he and his white companions turned to the southward. The successful Chickasaws danced around the flames in which they burned D'Artaguette, Vincennes and the Jesuit Senat, a priest who stayed and died of his own free will, because duty bade him.*

In the year 1729 Louisiana became the theater of a succession of tragedies at once both sickening and appalling, and between the inimical Indians and the French, many scalps were taken, and much blood was shed, until 1740, when a treaty of peace was concluded.

Very little is told us as happening between the years 1740 and 1750 in Western history. We give below some extracts from letters written by a missionary among the Illinois, which will serve to show the advancement of civilization in

* Western Annals, pp. 62, 63.

HISTORY OF OGLE COUNTY. 9

Letters from a Missionary—Settlements on the Mississippi—Lead Mines in Illinois—Their Value.

1750. Writing from "Aux Illinois," eighteen miles from Fort Rosalie, on the 8th of June, 1750, Vivier says: "We have here, whites, negroes, and Indians, to say nothing of the cross-breeds. There are five French villages, and three villages of the natives within a space of 21 leagues, situated between the Mississippi and another river called the Karkadiad (Kaskaskia.) In the five French villages are perhaps eleven hundred whites, three hundred blacks, and some sixty red slaves or savages. The three Illinois towns do not contain more than eight hundred souls, all told."

Vivier mentions in another part of the same letter Peoria, which probably contained as many inhabitants as the other three towns together. "Most of the French till the soil," he continues; "they raise wheat, cattle, pigs and horses, and live like princes. Three times as much is produced as can be consumed, and great quantities of grain and flour are sent to New-Orleans." Under date of November 17th of the same year, he writes: "For fifteen leagues above the mouth of the Mississippi one sees no dwellings, the ground being too low to be inhabited. Thence to New-Orleans the lands are only partially occupied. New-Orleans contains, black, white and red, not more, I think, than twelve hundred persons. To this point come all kinds of lumber, brick, salt beef, tallow, tar, skins and bear's grease, and above all, pork and flour from Illinois. These things create some commerce; forty vessels, and more, have come here this season. Above New-Orleans, plantations

are again met with; the most considerable is a colony of Germans, some ten leagues up the river. At Point Coupee, thirty-five leagues above the German settlement, is a fort. Along here, within five or six leagues, are not less than sixty habitations. Fifty leagues farther up is the Natchez Post, where we have a garrison who are kept prisoners by their fear of the Chickasaws and other savages. Here at Point Coupee, they raise excellent tobacco. Another hundred leagues brings us to the Arkansas, where we have also a fort and garrison for the benefit of river traders. There were some inhabitants about here formerly, but in 1748 the Chickasaws attacked the post, slew many, took thirteen prisoners, and drove the rest into the fort. From the Arkansas to the Illinois, nearly five hundred leagues,[*] there is not a settlement. There should, however, be a good fort on the Ouabache, (Wabash,) the only path by which the English can reach the Mississippi. In the Illinois are numberless mines, but no one to work them as they deserve. Some individuals dig lead near the surface and supply the Indians and Canada. Two Spaniards now here, who claim to be adepts, say that our mines are like those of Mexico, and that if we would dig deeper, we would find silver under the lead. At any rate, the lead is excellent. There is also in this country copper mines beyond doubt, as from time to time large pieces are found in the streams.

---

*In most of the ancient French journals, distance is overrated, as in this instance. It is nearer five hundred miles than leagues.

10   HISTORY OF OGLE COUNTY.

Alleged Purchases at Logstown and Lancaster—Resisted by the Iroquois on the ground of Fraud.

CHAPTER IV.

We have heretofore followed the movements of the French, who were making bold advances and sustaining severe losses, while the English, although they were watching with the most jealous carefulness the operations of the French, were comparatively inactive. Previous to 1750, no English settlement had been made West of the Alleganies, although Great Britain claimed the territory from the Atlantic to the Pacific, on the ground that the right secured by the discovery of the coast was a title of ownership to the whole country; and she also claimed the interior by right of actual discovery and by her purchase of it from the Indian owners. Among the discoveries made by the English, we notice, first, that of John Howard, who, tradition says, left Virginia in 1742, crossed the Alleganies, and descended the Ohio in a canoe of buffalo skins to the Mississippi, where he was taken prisoner by the French. This is the first well authenticated account we have of the English explorations of the Ohio and Mississippi. Six years after, Conrad Weiser was sent from Philadelphia to Logstown, an Indian village on the Ohio, to gain the friendship of the Western savages by presents and professions of good will toward them. There had doubtless been English traders along the Ohio some time previous to this expedition of Weiser; indeed, we have reason to believe that they had penetrated so far, as early as 1725, although there is no evidence which fixes the earliest date with any certainty. The country west of the Al-

leganies had, for a long time, to a great extent, been under the power of the Iroquois, a combination of six nations, who had by virtue of war gained possession of what is now Kentucky, Indiana, Ohio, Illinois, Wisconsin, some of British America, and even beyond the Mississippi. In 1684, at a treaty meeting held at Albany, this confederacy placed itself under the protection of the British government, and sold to the English a vast tract of country south and east of the Illinois River, and extending across Lake Huron into Canada."* The six nations, also, in 1726, signed a deed which placed their lands in the possession of the British, "to be protected and defended by his Majesty to and for the use of their heirs."† France by the treaty of Utrecht had agreed not to invade the country of Britian's Indian allies, and she certainly was justified in expecting the French to respect their obligations, and in claiming her own even by force of arms. The question of the extent of the possessions of the Iroquois arises here, which, with the claim of prior discovery by the French, leaves it a matter of investigation, whether or not the claims of the English were right, which we purpose to leave to others more curious.

Some of the country in question is said to have actually been purchased by the British, which fact was also put forward to substantiate their claim. This purchase was made at Lancaster, Pennsylvania, at a council which commenced its

*Western Annals.
†Powell's Administration of the Colonies, page 267.

session on the 22d of June, 1744, and lasted until the fourth of July. At this Convention the Commissioners from Maryland paid for the land purchased £220, in Pennsylvania currency; and those from Virginia paid £200 in gold and as much goods, promising more as settlements extended.* It was to fulfil this promise, as well as to "prospect" for settlements in the West, that Weiser made his expedition in 1748. France made every possible effort to drive back her rival without resorting to open war. In 1749, M. de Gallissoniere sent a party of soldiers under Louis Celeron, to place leaden plates, on which were inscribed at length the claims of France, in the mounds and at the mouths of the rivers† in the disputed territories, which, with various other plans to establish their claims, proved unavailing.

Companies were formed to colonize the West, which met with British support without regard to French claims. In 1748, the "Ohio Company" presented their petition to the king for a grant of land beyond the mountains, in answer to which petition the Governor of Virginia was directed to grant to the company a half a million acres of land beyond the mountains, in the Virginia Province. We find in the list of the members of this company, the name of George Washington, then little known to fame. The

Loyal Company received a grant of eight hundred thousand acres of land, on the 12th of June, 1749; and on the 29th of October, 1751, the Green Briar Company received a grant of one hundred thousand acres.

Thus the clouds were gathering for the storm, the conflicting elements in which were none other than the two proudest nations of the Old World, whose stage of action was this whole broad continent. The French fanned the flame already kindled in the breasts of the red men against their eastern invaders, while the English showed that stern determination which only is attended with success. The French in 1759 began to strengthen certain points on the Upper Ohio, from which the lower posts might be easily attacked, and opened a line of communication from Erie to the Allegany, on which road, at the head of French Creek, they built a fort. Early in 1752, the French demanded of the Twigtwees, a nation friendly to the English, the surrender of some traders who were established on the Miami, in the Twigtwees' country. These Indians could not thus easily be frightened to deliver their friends into the hands of their enemies, and consequently an attack ensued. Assisted by the Ottawas and Chippewas, after a severe battle, in which fourteen of the natives were killed and many more wounded, the French captured the post and carried the traders to Canada as prisoners.*

This was the result of the first attempt of the English to establish a permanent

---

*The alleged purchase at Logstown was sturdily resisted by the Iroquois, as also the Lancaster treaty claim, as a *fraud*. It was *never* admitted by the tribes of the Six Nations. See a tract called "Plain Thoughts."

†See Records of American Antiquarian Society, vol. 2, page 535—41.

*An early writer, speaking of this attack, says the prisoners were buried alive.

12   HISTORY OF OGLE COUNTY.

English Settlements West of the Mountains—The "Seven years War"—Grievances of the Colonists.

settlement west of the mountains. Blood had been shed; the French grew more zealous to blockade every avenue of approach, and the British, with a more fixed determination, prepared for the coming contest. Crown Point, Niagara, Riviere de Boeuf and the junction of the Monongahela and Allegany Rivers immediately became the sites upon which were located French forts, which were speedily garrisoned, and the Governors of the American provinces were commanded to drive away the French intruders from these posts by force of arms. In the same year, 1754, Washington, with four hundred men, was sent from Virginia to establish military works on the banks of the Ohio. Every American history has enlarged upon the achievements of this period, and it is scarcely necessary for us to repeat them. General Braddock soon arrived with a large force, and the seven years' war was fairly commenced. Speaking in this connection, Hart, in his "History of the Valley of the Mississippi," says:

"This war was ostensibly begun to assert the rights of each nation to the territory west of the mountains, but it was, in fact, a contest for supremacy throughout all the North American dominions. It began amidst the mountain-passes of the Alleganies; it ended on the Plains of Abraham. The struggle was not of long duration, but it was effectual, and afforded a convincing proof of the valor and prowess of the English soldiers, and their superiority over their French opponents. Nor in this trial of arms are we to obliterate the memory of the services which the old English colonists of America rendered to their ancestors in their endeavors to destroy French domination in this country. How far they were repaid for their services, history has not failed to mention; and while the memory of their achievements will forever be fixed in the minds of their countrymen, it will be accompanied by the melancholy reflection that they afterwards met with nothing but contumely and insult from that very power on whose behalf they were enlisted. The course of time and the progress of events have wiped away many of those asperities which formerly existed between the people of America and the mother country; and neither the one nor the other can ever obliterate from the hearts of Americans the memory of those unrequited services, which their gallant ancestors rendered in behalf of England in the wild solitudes of the West.

"It was neither the 'Stamp Act' nor the 'Tea Duty' which aroused the sense of wrong at the hands of England among the American people. These may have been the proximate cause, but there were others more remote which served to increase that feeling of indignation at the evils they had endured from their hard task-masters. The Colonists contracted a debt of ten millions to assist England in the war of 1754, and, if we may judge from the remonstrances of our ancestors, whose memorials were sent home to the British Parliament, they felt the ingratitude of England in withholding payment of this debt, and the recognition of more brilliant exploits they had performed during the memorable period."

We have said that the "seven years' war" was fairly commenced, and indeed, it was, although not formally declared until the following year, 1756. The story of the arrival of Braddock, his assuming command of all the British forces, including those of the colonies, his unskilful management and unhappy defeat, his burial in the road, although it forms an important link in our history as occuring the year previous to the Declaration of War, is too familiar to need delineation.

HISTORY OF OGLE COUNTY. 13

The treaty ratified at Paris—England possessor of the Colonies on the Atlantic, Canada and part of Louisana.

The destruction of life now became the employment of the living, and conspicuous among the annals of this period are the records of the gallant deeds of Wolfe and his brave companions, the destruction of Fort Duquesne, Washington's march through the Chestnut Ridge and the hazardous defence of Lewis and Bullitt, the fall of Montcalm, one of the bravest and noblest Frenchman of the age, before British bayonets at Quebec, the surrender of Montreal and the massacre of Michilimackinac—the details of these, time and space forbid our repeating.

On the 16th of February, 1762, a treaty was ratified at Paris by virtue of which England became possessor, not only of the colonies on the Atlantic, but the Canadas and that part of Louisiana lying east of the Mississippi, excepting the town of New-Orleans and the adjacent territory. In consideration of Havana and a greater part of Cuba, which the British had conquered, they, by the same treaty, acquired the Floridas from Spain. By a *secret* treaty of the same date, the country lying West of the Mississippi, and which was designated by the general appellation of Louisiana, was ceded by France to Spain.*

It will be seen that this treaty, vague and ambiguous in its terms, gave rise to constant collisions between the subjects of the European governments, and was the source of almost endless discussions

*The terms of this secret treaty have never been made known. On the third day of the preceding November, France ceded to Spain all her territories on the west side of the river, including the island and town of New-Orleans, which cession was accepted by the latter power on the 18th of the same month.—*Hart's History.*

between the authorities of our own government and Spain; for, by the treaty of 1762, Great Britain ceded East Florida, and guaranteed West Florida to the crown of Spain.

Hart says:

"In the phraseology of diplomatists, nothing could have been more uncertain than the limits assigned by the treaty of 1763. The right of navigating the Mississippi was for a long time a disputed point between England and Spain, and the space of twelve years was consumed in negotiating upon that and other subjects of boundary. It appears strange, that in the furthest recesses of the forest, where settlements originated out of that spirit of enterprise and industry which animated the bosoms of the early pioneers, their interests should have been so seriously affected by the wily intrigues of skilful diplomatists, but so it was; and we have seen that even the case of Langlade,* the English government had to

*Etherington, a British major, who was in possession of Fort Mackinac, April, 1763, gave authority to the Langlade family, of French descent, to make their permanent residence at Green Bay. Lieutenant Governor Sinclair repeated this permission in 1782. Founded under the auspices of the French government, encouraged and sanctioned by the rigorous and arbitrary power of the British crown, this, an infant settlement of the now populous State of Wisconsin, became so firmly rooted that to this day the descendants of Sieur Augustin de Langlade, who became the principal proprietor of the post of Green Bay in 1750, are living there; and the succeeding generations have preserved uncorrupted the polished manners and pure idiom of their native tongue, brought hither from the French court by their educated and high-minded ancestor.

We mention in this connection the settlement of Prairie du Chien, which, with that of Green Bay, dates its rise from the middle of the eighteenth century, and the other settlements of Wisconsin which we have incidentally or otherwise referred to, all of which increased in wealth and population, and now some of these are the most prominent locations in the State. Minnesota, too, the youngest member of our Confederacy, was the wonted field of the pale-face, who wandered over its fertile plains in quest of the prey which had long been that of the red man, and her earliest settlements date as far back as 1750, a few years previous to which time her soil was first broken by L'Huilier on the banks of the Mankato, who with his pickaxe and spade undertook to find vast beds of copper which he imagined were lying under her surface. Captain Jona-

grant permission to the subject of a foreign government to take up his abode on the shores of Lake Superior. The right of occupation, acquired after long years of toil and hardship, was by them considered subordinate to that which had been gained in war and on the battle field.

"Have we not reason to be thankful for the enlightened spirit and policy of our own free institutions which guaranteed to the stranger as well as to the native the protection of our laws and government? Yet such was the policy pursued by the European government in many periods of their political existence, that aliens were not allowed to abide in the country without the special permission of the crown. Such, however, does not seem to have been the case under the cession of Louisiana to Spain. It will be remembered that this secret treaty was not the result of any warlike operations between the two governments, and thus the Catholics inhabitants of Louisiana seemed to be the objects of the special care, and solicitude of the French monarch.

"In a letter signed by the French King, dated April 21st 1764, addressed to M. D'Abbadie, Director-General and Commandant of Louisiana, he informs him of the treaty of cession, and directs him to give up to the officers of Spain the country and colony of Louisiana, together with the city of New-Orleans' and all the military posts. He expressed a desire for the prosperity and peace of the inhabitants of the Colony and his confidence in the affection and friendship of the king of Spain, He at the same time declared his expectation that the ecclesiastical and religious bodies, who had the care of the parishes and missions, would continue to exercise their functions; that the Superior Council and ordinary Judges would continue to administer according to the laws,

forms and usages of the Colony; that the inhabitants would be maintained and preserved in their estates, which had been granted to them by the Governors and Directors of the Colony, and that finally, all these grants, though not confirmed by the French authorities, would be confirmed by his Catholic Majesty.

"Although this letter was dated April, 1764, it was not until the year 1768 that Spain exercised any permanent jurisdiction over the territory thus acquired by her.

"In the year 1766, Don Ulloa arived with a detachment of Spanish troops, and demanded possession of M. Aubey, the successor of D'Abbadie, who was deceased. This functionary, aided by the people, opposed the design of Spain. They complained that a transfer without their consent was unjust, and, in a moment of irritation, resorted to their arms, and obliged the Spaniards to measure their steps to Havana."

On the 17th of August, O'Reilly arrived from the East and took possession of the Colony without a show of resistance. By his authority six of the malcontents, who had been prominent in the measures of 1766, were immediately hung, and six more were doomed to the dungeons of Cuba.

The French established their settlements in Upper Louisiana, on the west branch of the Mississippi in 1766, one of which was the foundation of the present city of St. Louis; these were subjected to Spanish rule in 1770.

For years succeeding the signing of the secret treaty, the government of Spain in the Southwest presents a series of panoramic changes, interesting but painful to contemplate, and which fall just beyond the scope of our present undertaking.

---

than Carver also explored this country in 1766, and claimed a settlement from a gift which he pretends to have received from the Indians; and among those of the present century whom we are to regard as pioneers in promoting the early and rapid settlement, and who are prominent among the early explorers of this territory, stand the names of Cass and Schoolcraft, Nicolet, Fremont and Long.

Balanced, as it were, between the two great powers of Europe in the West, the Indian tribes of this country had been flattered and coaxed, hired and befriended by both parties, each in the hope of gaining a predominance of power by inducing them to become its allies; and when, for a passing period, either had been more successful, it was not slow to place in their hands European implements of warfare, and to instruct them in European arts of destruction. When, therefore, Great Britain was the only power to be met in the defence of their sacred hunting grounds, and when they could clearly perceive that, should that power consult its own best interests, the final extermination of their race must be inevitable, they were prepared to strike with effect the blow, which, should it be successful, would leave to them the boundless fields which the Great Spirit had given them. Illy did they count the cost of measuring arms with the British Lion.

Pontiac, an Indian Chief, whose name will ever stand among those of Logan, Blackhawk, Tecumseh, Philip and the like, in the archives of American history, succeeded, after the peace of 1763, in banding against the common foe, the Hurons, the Ottawas, the Chippewas and the Pottawatomies of the North, and the Shawnees, the Sakies, the Cherokees and several other prominent nations of the South, to extirpate from the land, whether by fair or foul means, these their enemies who had made such startling inroads upon the interior.

The author of "Western Annals" says: "The voice of their sagacious chief was heard in the North, crying, 'Why, says the Great Spirit, do you suffer these dogs in red clothing to enter your country and take the land I have given you? Drive them from it; drive them. When you are in distress, I will help you.' That voice was heard, but not by the whites. The unsuspecting traders journeyed from village to village, the soldiers in the forts shrunk from the sun of early summer, and dozed away the days; the frontier settler, singing in fancied security, sowed his crop, or, watching the sunset through the girdled trees, mused upon one more peaceful harvest, and told his children of the horrors of the ten years' war, now, thank God! over. From the Alleganies to the Mississippi the trees had leaved, and all was calm life and joy. But through that country, even then, bands of sullen red men were journeying from the central valleys to the lakes and the eastern hills. Bands of Chippewas gathered about Michilimackinac. Ottawas filled the woods near Detroit. The Maumee post, Presque Isle, Niagara, Pitt, Ligednier, and every English fort was hemmed in by mingled tribes, who felt that the great battle drew nigh which was to determine their fate, and the possession of their noble lands. At last the day came. The traders everywhere were seized, their goods taken from them, and more than one hundred of them put to death. Nine British forts yielded instantly, and the savages drank, 'scooped up in the hollow of their hands,' the blood of many a Briton. The border streams of Pennsylvania and Virginia ran red again. 'We hear,' says a letter from Fort Pitt, 'of scalping every hour.' In Western Virginia, twenty thousand people were driven from their homes."

As speedily as possible, a force was sent to the West under Maj. George Rogers Clark, and with him Pontiac signed a treaty of peace, which, however, on his part, was only an act of deception. Despite his tricks and traps, the three most prominent forts of the West were unconquered in the fall of 1763; old animosities among the Indians revived; gradually their ranks became disjointed and broken, and Pontiac, with a few followers, was incapable of completing the task so courageously began. The British government, having taken conciliatory steps towards those whom she acknowledged, had, in many cases been defrauded of their rights, a treaty of peace was concluded at Detroit, on the 21st of August, 1764, when more than twenty tribes were present, all of whom sued for peace. Subsequently very little of importance was effected by hostile Indians under the great Chief, while treaties were being made through the whole Northwest by which peace was being secured.

Pontiac was killed by a Kaskaskian Indian while in the act of rallying his dismembered army at a "Great Council." At the beginning of the difficulties between the Colonies and the mother country, Shegenata, the son of Pontiac, who in his youth had saved the life of a young Virginian who had wandered in the woods, and had lost his way, notwithstanding the endeavors of Hamilton, the Governor of Detroit, to frighten him from his purpose by telling him that only assassination would await him, appeared before the Virginia deputies, where, after reciving many presents and warm professions of friendship, he addresssed them as follows:

"Fathers, after the insinuations of the Commandent of Detroit, I accepted your invitation with distrust, and measured my route with trembling feet towards this 'Council of Fire'*

*A Council where he had come to light the calumnet of peace.

Your reception proves his falsehood, and that my fears were groundless. Truth and him have been a long time enemies. My father and many of my chiefs have lately tasted the bitterness of death.

The memory of this misfortune almost destroys my quality of man in filling my eyes with tears. Your sensible compassion has relieved my heart of this heavy burden, and the remembrance will be transmitted to the remotest posterity. Fathers, I rejoice at what I have just now heard, and I shall faithfully re late it to my nation. If for the future you wish to speak with me, I shall return with pleasure, and I thank you for my present invitation. The particular friendship which you expressed toward me, and the gun which you have given me for the care I took of your young friend Field, exact my most heartfelt gratitude. I feel that I did nothing but my duty. He who simply does his duty merits no praise. If any one of your nation should visit mine, either from curiosity or on business, or should be involuntarily thrust among us by the strong hand of the conqueror, he will ever meet the same reception which your brother received. You have assured me that if my nations hould visit yours, they 'will be welcome. My fears have ceased. I have no longer any doubts. I will recommend our young men to visit yours and make their acquaintance. Fathers, what has passed this day is too profoundly engraved on my heart for time ever to efface it. I predict that the sun's rays of this day of peace will warm the children of our children, and will protect them against the the tempests of misfortune. As a guarantee of what I say, I present you my right hand—this hand, which has never been given without the heart consented, which has never shed human blood in peace, nor spared an enemy in war; and I assure you of my friendship with a tongue which has never jested with truth, since I have been of that age to know that falsehood is a crime."

HISTORY OF OGLE COUNTY. 17

Progress of the Settlements—French Machinations among the Indians—Beginning of the Revolution.

With that spirit of progress which has ever characterized the English pioneers of early history, bold men were continually pressing forward to the Ohio and Mississippi, and making practical discoveries in the West. Among the earlier of these are the names of Geo. Croghan, whose expedition terminated in 1765, Ebenezer, Silas and John Zanes of 1769, and somewhat later, of Boone, Henderson, Lowther, Finley, Bullitt and McAfees; while, notwithstanding the many treaties of peace, single and combined tribes of Indians were holding in terror of the tomahawk, the whole power of advancing civilization. Drops of ink on parchment and paper might conciliate the executive of governments, but could not heal the sores that were made at Quebec and Pittsburg, or render an equivalent for the wounded pride of the French inhabitants from the "seven years' war." These were continually instigating the natives against the pioneers, and many a life was taken to satisfy their malice. It was not, however, French instigation that led to the memorable battle at the juncture of the Kanawha with the Ohio, so much as injustice on the part of the colonists toward those Indians with whom they were in a state of professed peace. In this battle, which took place on the 10th of October, 1774, there were no less than 215 killed and wounded of the colonial army, including among the killed three Colonels, five Captains, three Lieutenants and several subalterns. The loss of the Indians could not be estimated, as the bodies of their dead were immediately thrown into the Ohio. It must, at all events, have been much greater than that of the whites, as they were at length compelled to seek safety in flight, which they would have been the last to do, had not their numbers been reduced to a hopeless extremity.

Peace was effected by Lord Dunmore, the traitor governor of Virginia, who was smoothing the way, that he might succeed in the plot of uniting the Indians with Great Britain against the Colonies.

CHAPTER V.

The first echo of the Revolutionary War had no sooner been heard from the hights of Bunker Hill, than British emissaries filled the West, and by presents, fair promises, stratagems, and what not, endeavored to persuade the Indians to join them in their unholy cause. At first, the answer they met was:

"Look, the flames of war are kindled between men of the same nation. They are disputing among themselves for the hunting grounds which they have taken from us. Why should we embrace their quarrels? And what friend, what enemy shall we choose? When the red men carry on war, do the white men come among us to take part with one or the other? No, they allow our tribes to become weakened, and one to be destroyed by the other. They wait until the earth, bedewed with our blood, may lose its people, and become their inheritance. Let them, in their turn, exhaust their strength, and destroy themselves; we shall then recover, when they shall cease to exist, the forests, the mountains and lakes which belonged to our ancestors."

But not thus easily to be defeated in

3

their project, the tools of Britain persisted, and finally succeeded with the Iroquois, or "six nations," as well as with other tribes of the Northwest. The battle of Fort Stanwix, the rout of Bennington, the sad story of the almost entire extermination of the "Six Nations," the inhuman butchery of the peaceable Moravians, the murder of Cornstalk and its terrible results, the siege of Fort Henry, in which Captain Ogle rendered his bravery and coolness so conspicuous, when his numerous company fell around him, in the long and bloody conflict; Clark's march across this State, and his novel mode of reducing Kaskaskia, the capture of Cahokia, the changing fortunes of Fort Vincennes, and many other movements of this nature, connect in their narration the wily intrigues and savage inhumanity of Indian warfare, and examples of the most skillful generalship that the world has ever known, with the self-sacrificing bravery characteristic of the heroes of the Revolution. This bravery was not unrewarded; for on the 19th of April, 1784, a treaty of peace was concluded, and the red lion sent home to his den beyond the Atlantic. By this treaty, the line of division on the west ran through the center of the Mississippi, from its source to its mouth. Now, that this was effected, immigration began to pour into the country west of the Alleganies at a much more rapid rate than ever before, although single tribes of Indians continued to harass the frontiers, and every advancement must, as it were, be made in the face of death.

After Clark's successful march into the West, at which time many formerly hostile tribes became voluntarily the warmest friends, disavowing all connection with the British power, this country was formed into a county by the House of Burgesses of Virginia, and called Illinois, a name derived from a powerful tribe of Indians which inhabited her boundless prairies, October, 1778. A company, consisting of a few families from Virginia, made a settlement near Bellefontaine, in Monroe county, in 1784. This was the first settlement made in the country by people of the United States. St. Clair County may boast of the next American settlements, two of which were made previous to the year 1800. Speaking of pioneers, it may be pertinent to mention the Pittsburg *Gazette*, which was published in July 1788, being the first newspaper ever printed in the Northwest, and just eleven months later, the Kentucky *Gazette* was issued at Lexington. Let posterity remember the name of John Baptiste Trudeau, the western schoolmaster, who flourished at St. Louis as early as 1800. The honey-bee appeared on the banks of the Mississippi as early as 1792. In 1794, all the country east of the Mississippi and south of Canada was ceded by England to the United States. In 1800 Spain re-ceded Louisiana, and all the country on the west bank of the Mississippi, to the French Government, and the Emperor Napoleon, in 1803, disposed of it to the United States for $11,250,000. At the ceding of the Northwestern territory by Virginia to the United States in 1784, that country was placed under territorial gov-

HISTORY OF OGLE COUNTY. 19

General Arthur St. Clair appointed Governor of Indiana—Treaty with the Indians—Its Provisions.

ernment, and General Arthur St. Clair was appointed Governor of Indiana Territory, with which Illinois was connected for nine years.

It is impossible for us to give in detail a history of the depredations of the Indians on the frontier settlements, from the close of the Revolutionary War to the beginning of t' e War of 1812, although it embodies a tale of tragedy and romance, interesting but painful; yet the most prominent of these we propose to notice.

In the year 1804, was made the treaty between the United States and the united tribes of the Sacs and Foxes, and as the memorable Black Hawk War of 1832 was a violation of this treaty, we will give so ne of its conditions.

By Article 1st "the United States receive the Sacs and Fox tribes into their friendship and protection, and the said tribes agree to consider themselves under the protection of the United States, and no other power whatever."

By Article 2d, "the general boundary line between the lands of the United States and of the said Indian tribes, shall be as follows, viz: Beginning at a point on the Missouri River, opposite to the mouth of the Gasconade River; thence in a direct course, so as to strike the River Jefferson, to the Mississippi; thence up the Mississippi to the mouth of the Ouisconsin River, and up the same to a point which shall be thirty-six miles in a direct line from the mouth of said river; thence by a direct line to a point where the Fox River (a branch of the Illinois) leaves the small lake called the Sackaegan; thence down the Fox River to the Mississippi. And the said tribes, for and in consideration of the friendship of the United States, which is now extended to them, of the goods (to the value of two thousand two hundred and thirty-four dollars and fifty cents) which are now delivered, and of the annuity hereinafter stipulated to be paid, do hereby cede and relinquish forever to the United States all the lands included in the above described boundaries."

By Article 3d, "the United States agree to pay to these tribes $1,000 yearly in goods suitable to their wants, four hundred of which is to be delivered to the Foxes and six hundred to the Sacs."

By Article 4th, "the United States agree never to interrupt the said tribes in their peaceable possessions, but to protect them in their enjoyment of the same. In turn, these tribes agree not to sell their lands to any sovereign power but the United States, nor to the citizens or subjects of any sovereign power, nor to the citizens of the United States."

By Article 5th, "it is provided that for misconduct, on the part of individuals, there shall be no retaliation on the part of said individuals, but all difficulties shall be referred to the proper authorities, viz the Superintendent of Indian Affairs, or his Deputy, and the Chiefs of the said tribes, whose duty it shall be to inflict the necessary punishments, for the proper fulfilment of which, the said Superintendent, or Chiefs, were personally responsible."

Article 6th prohibits the settlement of any white man upon the Indian territo-

20   HISTORY OF OGLE COUNTY.

Provisions of the Treaty—"Additional Article"—Temporary Peace—Tecumseh's Scheme.

ry, and provides for the speedy removal of any who might do so.

Article 7th insures the right of the Indians to reside on the lands ceded to the United States, as long as those lands remain the property of the United States.

In Article 8th, the Indians promise not to allow any trader to reside among them without a license from the Superintendent of Indian Affairs, and also from time to time to give account, to the Superintendent or his Deputy, of such traders as may be among them.

By Article 9th, "the Government promises to establish a trading-house, where the individuals of said tribes may be supplied with goods at a reasonable rate, and thus be secured against the impositions of traders."

In Article 10th, "the Indians promise that a meeting of the representative Chiefs of the Osages and of the Sacs and Foxes shall take place to bury the tomahawk and renew friendly intercourse, and thus to establish peace on a firm and lasting basis between those nations which have so long been at war."

Article 11th provides for the building of military posts at the mouth of the Mississippi, or on the right bank of the Mississippi, and also secures the right of persons traveling through their country, to do so without molestation or taxation.

Article 12th states that this treaty shall be obligatory when ratified by the President and Senate of the United States.

Signed at St. Louis, Nov. 3d, 1804, by William Henry Harrison, and the Chiefs and head men of the said Sac and Fox tribes.

To these there is an "Additional Article," which reads as follows: "It is agreed that nothing in this treaty contained shall affect the claim of any individual, or individuals, who may have obtained grants of land from the Spanish Government, and who are not included within the general boundary line laid down in this treaty; provided that such grants have at any time been made known to the said tribes, and recognized by them."

Such is a summary of the treaty of 1804, which we have given thus at length, in order that it may be useful for reference.

A temporary peace having thus been secured, the inhabitants of Illinois were little molested until the outbreak of the War of 1812, when the West again became the theater of exciting action. Tecumseh, a man far famed in history, seeing the foundation of existence for his countrymen crumbling beneath them, aware of the terrible results to the common foe of united effort, as effected under Pontiac and other renowned chiefs before him, laid the foundation of a scheme, which, if it had been successful in its execution, would have lengthened out the being of that strange race, whose last feeble remnants are fast sinking away upon the borders of the Pacific. His plan was, to unite in one grand compact all those tribes which had any intercourse whatever with the United States; and his object was, by this compact to prevent any sale of lands belonging to these tribes to the United States, and to introduce among the savages the arts of civilized nations, and thus to obtain the security derived from civilization.

"Tecumseh entered upon the great work he had in contemplation, in the year 1805 or 1806. He was then about thirty-eight years of age. To unite the several Indian tribes, many of whom were hostile to, and had often been at war with each other, in this great and important undertaking, prejudices were to be overcome, their original customs and manners to be re-established, the use of ardent spirits to be abandoned, and all intercourse with the whites to be suspended. The task was herculean in its character, and beset with difficulties on every side. Here was a field for a display of the highest moral and intellectual powers. He had already gained the reputation of a brave and sagacious warrior, and a cool headed, upright, wise and efficient counselor. He was neither a war nor peace Chief, and yet he wielded the power and influence of both. The time having arrived for action, and knowing full well that, to win savage attention, some bold and striking movement was necessary, he imparted his plan to his brother, the Prophet, who adroitly, and without a moment's delay, prepared himself for the part he was appointed to play in the great drama of savage life. Tecumseh well knew that excessive superstition was everywhere a prominent trait in the Indian character, and, therefore, with the skill of another Cromwell, brought superstition to his aid.

"Suddenly, his brother began to dream dreams and see visions; he became afterwards an inspired prophet favored with a divine commission from the Great Spirit—the power of life and death was placed in his hands—he was appointed Agent for preserving the property and lands of the Indians, and for restoring them to their original happy condition. He thereupon commenced his sacred work. The public mind was aroused, unbelief gradually gave way; credulity and wild fanaticism began to to spread its circles, widening and deepening, until the fame of the prophet, and the divine character of his mission, had reached the frozen shores of the lakes, and overrun the broad plains which stretch far beyond the great Father of Waters. Pilgrims from remote tribes sought, with fear and trembling, the headquarters of the prophet and the sage. Proselytes were multiplied, and his followers increased beyond all former examples. Even Tecumseh became a believer; and seizing upon the golden opportunity, he mingled with the pilgrims, won them by his address, and on their return, sent a knowledge of his plan of concert and union to the most distant tribes.

"The bodily and mental labors of Tecumseh now commenced. His persuasive voice was one day listened to by the Wyandots, on the plains of Sandusky; on the next, his commands were issued on the banks of the Wabash. He was anon seen paddling his canoe across the Mississippi; then boldly confronting the Governor of Indiana in the Council House at Vincennes; now carrying his banner of union among the Creeks and Cherokees of the South, and from thence to the cold and inhospitable regions of the North, neither intoxicated by success nor discouraged by failure."*

As the clouds of war again began to gather upon the political horizon of our country, the old measures of Great Britain, which in the days of '76 covered her noblest conquests with the foulest stains, began again to be put into operation, and three years before the opening of hostilities, British officers were again stirring up to deeds of deep resentment the red men on the frontiers, and instiling into their minds the belief that the sovereignty over all the country not ceded in the treaty of Greenville, ought to be theirs. The minds of Tecumseh and the Prophet were ripe for lessons of this nature, for through them was opening up a seeming foundation to justify the prose-

*Brown's History of Illinois.

22   HISTORY OF OGLE COUNTY.

Treaties Made—Battle of Tippecanoe—Formation of Illinois Territory—Government of Illinois.

cution of their daring project. Awake to the kindling flame, Governor Harrison, in an address to these two brothers, says:

"Brothers, I am myself of the Long Knife fire; as soon as they hear my voice, you will see them pouring forth their swarms of 'hunting shirt men,' as numerous as the musquitoes on the shores of the Wabash. Brothers, take care of their sting."

Treaties were effected and purchases made so that our claims to the western territory might be founded on principles of equity. Of those from whom land was bought were the Chippewas, Ottawas, Pottawatomies, Wyandots, Shawnees, Delawares, Miamis, Eel River Indians, Weas and Kickapoos.

The first battle, of very great importance, which occurred as the fruit of the schemes of Tecumseh and the Prophet, was that of Tippecanoe, on the upper waters of the Wabash. The particulars of this disastrous engagement are given at length in almost every American History, so that we need not recapitulate.

Tecumseh and his friends united with the British in the War of 1812; and fought and died with the bravery of desperation, for with the memorable defeat of his army at the battle of Tippecanoe, his hope of success in his magnificent enterprise seemed to have died within him, and we have good reason to believe that the sequel would have proved far more disastrous to the whites, had he been present in person to superintend the events of that period.

That country lying to the west of Indiana, and known by the name of Illinois, was in 1809 formed into the "Illinois Territory," and Hon. Ninian Edwards, then Chief Justice of Kentucky, was appointed Governor, and Nathaniel Pope, Esq. of Kaskaskia, Secretary of the Territory.

The history of the government of Illinois, up to 1809, runs as follows: Originally, and under French control, Illinois was a portion of ancient New-France. About the year 1715 or 1720, it was made a part of the colony of Louisiana. By the treaty of 1763, in connection with Canada, this country was ceded to British authority. By authority of this power, Captain Sterling established the Provisional Government at Fort Chartres, in 1765. The following year, by virtue of the Quebec Bill, Illinois, and the whole Northwestern territory, was placed under the local supervision of Canada. Thus it remained two years, when the conquest of the country, by General Clark, placed it under the jurisdiction of Virginia, which, in October, 1778, organized the county of Illinois. The country was ceded to the Continental Congress in 1784, but the ordinance providing for a Territorial Government was not passed until 1787, and its provisions were not acted upon until 1788; and in 1789 Governor St. Clair organized the county that now bears his name. This had been a part of Indiana Territory from 1800, at which time the government was of two grades; the first constituting the law making power, and consisting of the Governor and Judges; the second grade was the Territorial Legislature, consisting of a House of Representatives elected by the people, and a Council appointed by the President and Senate. Previous to 1812, the Territorial Government of Illinois was of the first grade.

The year 1811 is distinguished as the one in which was built the *New-Orleans,* the first steamboat ever built beyond the Alleganies. In 1817 the *General Pike* was built. This steamboat, which was the first to navigate the upper waters of the Mississippi, arrived at St. Louis in the year above mentioned; and in 1819 the *Independence* was built to ply on the Missouri, and ascended as far as Franklin and Chariton.

On the 28th of April, 1809, Nathaniel Pope, acting Governor, issued his proclamation dividing the Territory of Illinois into two counties—Randolph and St. Clair. These were the only counties in the Territory for the three years preceding 1812.

On the 14th of February, 1812, Governor Edwards ordered an election to be held in each county, on the second Monday of April, that the people might decide whether they would enter upon the second grade of government. It was in the power of the Governor to advance the territory to the second degree, but he chose to be guided by the popular will. The people, by a very large majority, decided the question in the affirmative.

In September of the same year, the Governor organized the counties of Madison, Gallatin, Pope and Johnson; and at the same time authorized an election to be held on the 8th, 9th and 10th days of October, to elect members of the Council and House of Representatives.*

* Western Annals.

Pursuant to the Governor's proclamation, the first Territorial Legislature assembled at Kaskaskia on the 25th of November, 1812. Benjamin Talbot of Gallatin county, William Biggs of St. Clair county, Samuel Judah of Madison county, and Pierre Menard of Randolph county, took their seats as members of the Council. The following gentlemen took their seats as members of the House: George Fisher, Randolph county; Philip Trommel and Alexander Wilson, Gallatin county; John Grammor, Johnson county; Joshua Oglesby and Jacob Short, St. Clair county, and William Jones of Madison county.

On the night of the 16th of December, 1811, commenced a series of earthquakes, which continued until the following February. In these, the town of New-Madrid was almost entirely destroyed; the banks of the Mississippi, in many places, gave way in large masses and fell into the river, while the waters changed to a reddish hue, became thick with mud thrown up from the bottom, and the surface, lashed violently by the agitation of the earth beneath, was covered with foam, which gathered into masses and floated along on the trembling surface. Its vibrations were felt all over the valley of the Ohio, as far up as Pittsburg.*

In the year 1712 occurred the massacre of Chicago. A small trading post had been established at this point by the French, but no village had been formed. By the treaty of Greenville, in 1795, the Indians had relinquished a piece of land

* Dr. Hildreth.

24　　　HISTORY OF OGLE COUNTY.

The Massacre at Chicago—Dispatches from Gen. Hull—Attack by the Indians.

six miles square, at the mouth of Chicago river. In 1804, a small fort was erected here by the United States Government, and called Fort Dearborn. In 1812, the fort was occupied by a small garrison, few of the men being effective. John H. Kinzie and his family were residing at the fort, as well as a few Canadians and their wives and children.

On the 17th of April, a band of Winnebagoes attacked Mr. Lee's settlement at Hardscrabble, about four miles from Chicago, and killed a Mr. White and a Frenchman in his employ. There were signs of hostile Indians for some days after this, but the whole passed off in quietness until all alarm had disappeared.

On the 17th of August, Winnemeg, a trusty Pottawatomie chief, arrived at the fort, with dispatches from General Hull, the Commander-in-chief in the Northwest. From these dispatches Captain Heald, commander of the fort, learned that war had been declared between England and the United States; that General Hull, at the head of the army in the Northwest, was on his way from Fort Wayne to Detroit; and that the British troops had taken Mackinac. General Hull's orders to Captain Heald were, "to evacuate the post, if practicable, and in that event, to distribute the property belonging to the United States, and in the fort, and in the factory or agency, to the Indians in the neighborhood."

After having delivered his dispatches, Winnemeg privately informed Mr. Kinzie that he knew their contents, and strongly advised that the post should not be vacated. If it was to be done, however, he advised that it be done immediately, as the Indians were ignorant of his mission, and a forced march might be made through their country. Captain Heald, however, disregarded this advice, and resolved to carry out the orders he had received. By this means the Indians were informed of their intentions, and prepared to massacre them.

On the 13th, the goods were distributed, the extra ammunition being thrown into an old well, and the spirits poured upon the ground.

On the morning of the 15th of August, the party set out, accompanied by five hundred Pottawatomies, who had pledged their honor to escort them safely. On reaching a range of sand hills within the present limits of Chicago, the Pottawatomies defiled to the right, so as to bring the sand hills between them and the Americans. They had marched a mile and a half from the fort, when Captain Wells, who, with his Miamis, was in advance, rode back and exclaimed, "They are about to attack us; form instantly and charge upon them." He had scarcely finished speaking when a volley of balls was showered upon them. The troops charged up the bank, and the battle became general. The Miamis fled at the first onset, though Captain Wells used every endeavor to make them stand their ground. Overpowered by numbers, the whites surrendered after the loss of two-thirds of their force, stipulating for the preservation of their lives and those of the remaining women and children, and for their delivery at some of the British posts, unless ransomed by traders in

HISTORY OF OGLE COUNTY. 25

Revenue of Illinois in 1811-14—Admission into the Union—Julien Dubuque—Treaty of 1804.

the Indian country. Notwithstanding these stipulations, the wounded were horribly mutilated and inhumanly killed, and the children, twelve of whom were placed together in a baggage wagon, were butchered by the merciless savages. The next morning the fort was burned by the Indians. The prisoners were afterwards liberated.

In the Territorial Legislature of 1814, the Committee on Revenue reported that from January 1st, 1811, to November 8th, 1814, the revenue from taxes received was $4,875.45; of which there had been paid into the Treasury $2,516.89, and remained in the hands of delinquent Sheriffs, $2,378.47. As a matter for comparison, we may state here that the total amount collected for the various revenue purposes, in the State of Illinois, for the year 1858, was $4,867,792.90 !

On the 18th of April, 1818, the people of Illinois were authorized by Congress to form a State Constitution, and 42 deg. and 30 min. north latitude was fixed upon as the Northern boundary. For this purpose a convention assembled in July following, at Kaskaskia, where fifteen counties were represented, viz: Johnson, Edwards, St. Clair, Randolph, Madison, Gallatin, White, Monroe, Pope, Jackson, Crawford, Bond, Union, Washington and Franklin.

CHAPTER VI.

At a council with the Indians in 1786, Julien Dubuque procured a grant of 140,-000 acres of land, including the present city of Dubuque, near which lie the remains of this hardy pioneer.

In the possession of this grant, which, however, was to revert to the Indians at his death, he married an Indian woman, adapted himself to their style of life, and amassed immense wealth by mining and trading with them. Dubuque's first visit to the Upper Mississippi country was made as early as 1786. He died in 1810, and was buried about a mile below the present city of Dubuque, where his grave may still be seen.

In 1804, General Harrison purchased from the Sac and Fox Indian tribes, treating with Quash-que-ma, or Pumpkin Chief, a tract of land fifteen miles square, on the east side of the Mississippi, where the city of Galena is now situated. For this the Indians did not receive all their pay until 1829, and in this negligence may lie one of the causes which led to the War of 1812. As this action of Quash-que-ma was done without consulting Black Hawk, the great chief felt himself insulted; for he, as he had been aid-de-camp to the brave Tecumseh, was certainly a man of dignity, and was not thus to be passed over as a cypher in the prominent transactions of his nation. Dissensions therefore arose, and a temporary division was made. Keokuk, a cotemporary of Black Hawk, became chief of the southern portion of the nation, Black Hawk retaining supervision of the northern. They made yearly visits to the diggings, and thus having a good opportunity, they could watch the movements of the whites with all the carefulness that jealousy might dictate.

4

26   HISTORY OF OGLE COUNTY.

Trading Post on Fever River—Discovery of Galena Lead Mines—Early Pioneers in the Mining Region.

About the mouth of April, 1819, Jesse W. Shull established a trading post on an island a few miles above the mouth of the Mecapiasipo, the Indian name for Fever River. He was soon after informed that the Indians had discovered a lead near where Galena now stands, and as this promised to be something of importance—which proved true, as it turned out to be the noted "buck lead"—at the request of the Indians he moved down to the point. Here he was joined in the following summer, by Mr. A. P. Van Metre, and a little later by Dr. Samuel Mure, who has the honor of giving Galena its name.*

Previous, however, to either of these, a gentleman named Boutillier built and occupied a shanty on the east side of Fever River during the summer of 1819, and to him must be given the honor of being the first white inhabitant of Galena. In regard to the first settlements of the city and its vicinity, we quote from the matter-of-fact Red Clay correspondent of the Galena *Sentinel*, to whom we are indebted for much valuable information:

"In the fall of the year 1819, our old friend Captain D. G. B. started from St. Louis, with a French crew, for Fever River, Upper Mississippi Lead Mines. His vessel was a keel boat, the only way of conveyance, then, for heavy burthens on the Upper Mississippi, and boatmen in those days were some of them

'half horse, half alligator;' but the merry French, after arriving off Pilot Knob, commenced their march for Fever River. After a search of three days, they found the mouth; and on the 17th of November, after pushing through the high grass and rice lakes, they arrived safe at where Galena now stands, where they were greeted by some of the natives, from the tall grass, as well as by our old acquaintances, J. B. Shull and A. P. Van Metre, who had taken to themselves wives of the daughters of the land, and were traders for their brethren. They were received in the true spirit of the age. As the French have more tact with the Indian character than others, they caused feasting rather than envy. Dr. Mure, likewise, was just establishing a trading house; he had been induced, while in the army, to take a wife of the aborigines; associated with an Indian trader at Rock Island, Davenport, they made up the principal head men and chiefs now in the diggins with uncle Davy's crew. Captain B., after disposing of or leaving his cargo in exchange for lead, furs, &c., returned to St. Louis for another cargo.

"The next year he had awakened a spirit of enterprise. Col. J. Johnson, with no small pomp, for those days, had procured permission, either directly from the President or Secretary of War—as the war department sometimes assumes the prerogative here—(Mr. Calhoun, I think,) Col. J. claimed almost the exclusive privilege of mining. The Col. started with two large barges and some seventy men. Our friend Meeker had procured permission from headquarters to mine and smelt about this time. He was accompanied by Mr. Harris and family, B. Hunt, J. S. Miller and family, J. Smith, now at Dubuque. By this time our Capt B. has made a second trip, concludes to settle, turn into mining, merchandising and smelting. He formed an addition—Toulison, a Frenchman, A. Farran, and perhaps Harvey. They were closely allied to the Indians, and looked quite savage at Johnson's crew, Lieutenant Burdwine, having the appointment

*Doubtless from the Greek, *Galanas*, a name applied to a "particular species of lead-ore." Whether the mineral in the vicinity of Galena is the same as the "particular specie" to which the ancients applied this name, we are unable to say.

HISTORY OF OGLE COUNTY. 27

The "Suckers"—Discoveries by the Indians—Jesse W. Shull Bargains with them to work the Mines.

of Superintendent of Lead Mines, or acting as Superintendent. On his arrival here, Col. Johnson sent word to his camp, for him to repair to head-quarters. Uncle D. sent back word to Johnson, if he wanted to see him more than he did, to call; he declined the summons, and soon a file of men came to command his presence. But as Uncle Davy was one of those who had long been a boatman, he concluded to take his time. After dropping his boat below the point, he deliberately, after they had set up a shout that they had left, suddenly in the midst of their rejoicings, made his appearance, and informed Lieut. Burdwine, if he had any commands for him, he was at his 'sarvice.'

"I have been thus particular in the outset, at the commencement as well as the present, that my readers, if any, may see that at all times there has been a little extra *swell-work* of this pretended *sovereignty*. After a while, things settled down. Uncle Davy unpacked and commenced sales; tea, $5 a pound, coffee, $1, sugar, 75 cts.; all other articles in proportion.

"Now, I have got the early particulars of this year. In '23 and '24, a few more came—Captain Low, with a company of soldiers, stationed at Low's Point, from which it took its name. Addition 1st. John Connelly, the Indian Agent, established his office here. Some mining had been done. Col. Johnson worked the old 'Buck Lead,' and sowed a great deal of float, or gravel mineral, as I am told by his nephew, Matthew, to get the miners further out to mine and prospect. Johnson sold out some prospects—by it some leads were found. This I name, just as I had it from him."

There are a kind of fish which, in the spring of the year, run up the rivers and streams of our State, and often going as far north as the very source of the streams in which they may happen to be. These are called "suckers." So the people from the southern portion of the State used to come up to the Upper Mississippi with provisions for the miners, remaining through the summer, and returning in the fall; therefore, they were called "suckers," which, growing in the extent of its application, became the general name of the natives of the State.

Mr. Shull, in the fall of 1825, was informed by an Indian that he had found traces of lead beyond the limits of the tract sold to the whites, and that he would disclose it to him, providing that he should receive compensation for his services, and the privilege of working. His proposition was accepted, but after visiting the spot designated by the red skin, and finding nothing particularly attractive, Mr. Shull returned to Galena, where he remain until the following spring without taking any further notice of the Indian's discovery. Then he returned and found, after a little digging, an immense bed of lead. One day, while intently at work in his new-found mine, he happened to raise his eyes from his work, when he discovered a troop of Winnebagoes, headed by Wabokieshick, the prophet, coming toward him at full speed. They immediately commanded him to desist, asking him how he had dared to leave the proper boundaries of the whites, and trespass on their grounds. They told him that no *one* of their tribe had any right to sell the property of the nation, but as he was a friend, they would permit him to dig with them if he chose. With this, they all set to work, and soon rolled out several large blocks of the shining ore. After some bartering, Shull succeeded in purchasing the land in that

28   HISTORY OF OGLE COUNTY.

Land Titles—Troubles with the Indians—Visit to Winneshiek Village—Treaty with the Indians.

vicinity, and this was the commencement of the "Shullsburg diggings."*

In the summer of 1826, George Ferguson and Robert Clayton discovered the "New Diggings," and in the fall of the same year, "East Fork Diggings" were found. Captain Thomas, in 1827, surveyed the village, and the government permitted individuals to occupy and improve lots, provided they would surrender their claims on thirty days' notice from the proper authorities. This was the only title the citizens had for their land up to the year 1838.

CHAPTER VII.

The same restive spirit which has marked the character of the red man, ever since the pale-face was planted on American soil, was not yet quite asleep. The number of miners had, in 1827, increased to about sixteen hundred; and, proud of their numbers, they had committed some depredations well calculated to kindle the smouldering flame, besides trespassing beyond their own properly prescribed limits. The whites and Indians viewed each other with jealous eyes, and the latter only waited for an opportunity to show their ill-will. Finally, matters grew worse. A keel boat was attacked while passing down the Mississippi. The Indians murdered a family at Prairie du Chien; and when the murderers were demanded, they refused to give them up. It suddenly became apparent that a war could not be

*History of Stephenson County.

avoided, and the people in all parts of the mining country began to prepare for defence. Major General Gaines, in command of the regular troops, scoured the country, in order to learn what to expect from the Indians, and General Henry Dodge raised several companies of volunteers, and assisted in this work. In one of his expeditions, General Dodge visited the Winneshiek village, situated where the city of Freeport now stands, and found that the old chief, who had always been firm in his friendship to the whites, had gone with his band to attend the great council which, it was reported, was being held on the Wisconsin.

At the time of General Dodge's visit, the Winneshiek band numbered almost two hundred. The chief himself was near sixty years of age, and is described as "a short fleshy man, very taciturn, very honest, and, more wonderful than all for an Indian, very temperate." Winneshiek is still living at Blue Earth, Minnesota, and is about ninety years old.

Finding effective measures taken against them, the Indians began to retreat, as was supposed, for the Chippewa country. They were pursued up the Wisconsin to near Fort Winnebago, where they were overtaken. An attempt to meet the whites in a contest would be useless. They were more than a match for the Indians in arms and numbers. A treaty was made, by which they were to receive $20,000 for the damages they had sustained, and the whites were to be allowed to occupy a part of the mineral lands. Thus ended the Winnebago difficulty. "About a year afterwards, a large tract of mine-

HISTORY OF OGLE COUNTY. 29

Country Purchased—The Early Miners—Attempt to possess Dubuque's Mines—Next Neighbors.

ral country was purchased from the Indians. Two strips of land, the one extending along the Wisconsin and Fox rivers, from the east to the west, giving a passage across the country from Lake Michigan to the Mississippi, and the other reaching from Rock Island to the Wisconsin, were at the same time purchased."*

When the Winnebagoes were told that they must cross the Wisconsin, and at some not very far distant period the Mississippi also, because they and the whites could not live in peace together, they replied, "We have to do just as you say; we are now weak and cannot help ourselves; we once were a powerful nation. Those blue hills you see yonder used to echo far and wide with our war-cries, while the smoke of our council-fires ascended to the blue vault of heaven to the Great Spirit, the Father of the red man. But our bow is now unstrung, our hatchet is buried, our warriors sleep on yonder mounds; their leaf is withered, and the green turf covers their bosoms; our arrows sleep in the quiver. Tell our great father, the President, we must submit to his wishes."

The miners had no time to till the soil, and, as a consequence, were dependent on the provisions brought up the Mississippi. They were sometimes reduced to sore extremities, particularly when the navigation opened very late in the Spring. As a community, they were governed by such laws as would suit their particular emergencies; for when the commission of any crime occurred, they organized a

*History of Stephenson County.

court, proceeded to investigation, and administered such punishment as the exigency seemed to demand.

In 1829, an attempt was made by some Galena miners to take possession of Dubuque's old mining grounds, but they were frightened away by some one from St. Louis, who pretended to have claims against Dubuque's property; but when they afterwards learned that at Dubuque's death his interest there reverted to the Indians, and any other claim could not be sustained, they returned to the works, making such temporary arrangements with the Indians as from time to time might be required. Since the first movements in the Upper Mississippi Lead mines, a company had been formed consisting of Farnham, Davenport and Farrar, the first of whom had located a trading post at Flint Hills, now Burlington. The second, Col. Davenport, had established a post at Rock Island, and Farrar was the manager of the interests of the company, at Galena.

The next neighbors our Galena friends had, south of them, at the period of which we are speaking, were at Peoria; and between the two places was a vast wilderness of uninhabited territory, to the settlements of Vandalia and the region just about it. In 1830, this territory was here and there dotted with habitations which occupied the most attractive and inhabitable situations along the banks of the creeks and rivers. Settlers were sparsely located along the Mississippi up to Galena, and even the rough country above, sometimes at a distance of a hundred miles from each other; and, like-

30   HISTORY OF OGLE COUNTY.

Early Steamboat Navigation—First Grist Mill in the Northwest—Mails—First Newspapers—Protestant Missionaries.

wise, on the Illinois up to Chicago. The country lying between Galena and Chicago, embracing nearly one-third of the State, and the part, too, which is now regarded as most desirable for habitation, was yet to be peopled.

As the West thus began to open her resources to civilization, the institutions of civilization must of necessity follow in its train. The old manner of navigation by the slow and tedious keel-boats had to give way to the steamboats, of which, the first to ascend the river so far as the Des Moines Rapids, was the *Western Engineer*, in 1819. The *Virginia* was the first steamboat to touch at Galena. Thus early introduced, the navigation of the Mississippi by steam became a prominent feature of western improvement, and to it we are not a little indebted for the rapid strides of advancement in this portion of the country. But, living in so rich a country, it was poor policy for the miners to depend entirely upon importation for their subsistence. Grain was produce t which must be ground, and consequently grist-mills must be built; the first of these erected in the Northwest, was at Galena—a corn-cracker—the hopper containing about a peck, and the building containing it was a dry-goods box. Besides the mail coming up the river from St. Louis, a one horse mail was established from Galena to Vandalia, to pass over the route every two weeks; this was in 1826. The *Miners' Journal* was published at Galena, commencing July 4th, 1826, by James Jones, who, in 1832, sold out to Dr. Philleo, who changed the name to the *Galenean.* In 1829, Newhall, Philleo

& Co. commenced the publication of the *Galena Advertiser*, which is still a successful and popular newspaper in the hands of H. H. Houghton. In the southern portion of the State, the *Vandalia Intelligencer* commenced its publication about the time Vandalia was made the seat of government. Mr. Rice started the first school in the Northwest, at Galena, in 1829.

Rev. A. Kent, a Presbyterian missionary, arrived at Galena early in 1829; and about a week later, Rev. Mr. Dow, of the Methodist Episcopal Church, also came, and together they at once set about the great work before them. Four years later, a missionary arrived at Chicago. At their own expense, the early missionaries traversed the wilderness, slept in the open air, swam rivers, suffered cold and hunger, traveled on foot and on horseback, to preach the Gospel, to establish churches and schools, in short, to make the West what it now is, so far as their exertions have had any influence.

Rev. Mr. Kent commenced a school after two or three others had been started. He relates, as an incident of these school-teaching days, that on one occasion he had punished a girl for some infringement of the rules, and was brought before the usual tribunals on a charge of assault and battery, but was triumphantly acquitted. As an evidence that the former animosities have died away, Mr. K. says that he was recently called upon to perform the marriage ceremony for the same girl and her lover.

Chicago, up to 1829 or '30, was nothing more than a military station and tra-

HISTORY OF OGLE COUNTY. 31

Organization of the State Government—Population in 1818 and '80—Gov. Reynolds—Kellogg's Trail.

ding post of even less importance than Rock Island.

CHAPTER VIII.

The first Governor of the State was Shadrach Bond, who commenced his four years' term in October, 1818. He died about the year 1834, and the county of Bond was named for him. Ex-Governor Edwards and Jesse B. Thomas were the first United States Senators from Illinois. Elias K. Kane was appointed Secretary of State, Daniel P. Cook was elected the first Attorney-General, Elijah C. Berry Auditor of Public Accounts, and John Thomas State Treasurer. Mr. Cook was elected to Congress in 1818, and continued to serve in that body until 1827. To his services we are indebted for the donation by the General Government of 300,000 acres of land, for the construction of the Illinois and Michigan Canal. As a fitting tribute to his memory, the county in which Chicago is situated bears his name.

The first State Legislature convened at Kaskaskia in October, 1818. By the journals of this Legislature, we find that the committee appointed for the purpose purchased a sufficient stock of stationery at a cost of $13.50. One of the most remarkable laws passed by this Legislature was that relating to negroes and mulattoes, which contained all the most stringent provisions of similar acts in the slave States.*

*For a full summary of the provisions of this Act, see Ford, p. 32, et seq.

The population of Illinois, in 1818, was about 45,000, many of whom were descendants of the old French settlers. In 1830, the population had increased to 157,447.

In 1827, an exciting election for State Treasurer occurred in the Illinois Legislature, in which the former incumbent was defeated. Immediately after the adjournment of the General Assembly, and before the members had time to leave the house, the defeated candidate walked in and inflicted corporeal 'punishment' upon four of the members who had voted against him. No steps were taken to bring the offender to justice; but at the same session he was appointed clerk of the circuit court and recorder for Jo Daviess county, of which Ogle county then formed a part.

In August, 1830, John Reynolds was elected Governor. A new Legislature was elected at the same time. Ex-Gov-Reynolds was the candidate of the Buchanan wing of the Democratic party for Superintendent of Public Instruction, in the canvass of 1858.

CHAPTER IX.

In the spring of the year 1825, a Mr. Kellogg started from Peoria for the Upper Mississippi Lead Mines. Crossing Rock River a few miles above the present locality of Dixon, he passed up through the prairie lying between Polo and Mount Morris, touched the western part of West Grove, and continued northward to Galena. The way thus being opened, several others, during the summer and fall of the same year, some with teams, more on foot, all "camping out," passed over the route traveled by Kellogg, and thus was made what in those early days was called "Kellogg's Trail."

The method of crossing Rock River without bridge or ferry was very simple. The Winnebagoes and other Indians who were very numerous in this vicinity at the time, were thickly settled along the banks of the river, and were easily induced to assist the whites. Two of their canoes, placed side by side, formed a ferry-boat, the two wheels of one side of the wagon being placed in the one, and the two wheels of the opposite side in the other; they were thus safely and easily transported. The horses were made to swim over the river, and then all being safe on the opposite side, they were hitched up and proceeded on their way as before.

As "Kellogg's Trail" was somewhat circuitous, bearing too far east to be the nearest route, a Mr. John Boles, traveling across the country in the spring of 1826, left the beaten track some distance south of Rock River, crossed the river at Dixon, just above where the bridge of the I. C. R. R. is now placed, passed up through the country about a mile east of Polo, north, to White Oak Grove, a half a mile west of Foreston, thence through Crane's Grove, and so on to Galena. This being much preferable to the old way, it immediately became the traveled route and was called "Boles' Trail" This trail was used exclusively for the three years following, and may still be plainly seen a few miles east of Polo on the prairie.

In the season of 1826, the travel over the country was about double that of the summer and fall preceding.

Travel commenced again early in 1827. In the month of March of this year, Elisha Doty, now a citizen of Polo, came up from Dixon, attempted to cross the river on the ice, but before he had proceeded far the ice began to give way, and he was obliged to give up the attempt. He says that while waiting on the bank, just before starting on his return, about two hundred teams had collected there, all on the way to Galena. We mention this that a correct idea may be formed of the amount of travel to and fro through the country at this early period. Nor was this the only line of travel from Peoria and other southern settlements to Galena. The "Lewiston Trail," opened about the time of the "Kellogg Trail," passed some distance west of our county, and crossed Rock River a little above Prophetstown, in Whiteside county.

Isaac Chambers, the first white inhabitant of Ogle county, passing through the country to Galena early in the summer, was struck with the beauty of this particular vicinity, and determined to make it his future home.

The place where Dixon now stands had become a fixed place for travelers to cross the river, and much inconvenience was experienced in getting across, as the Indians were not always at hand, and it was unpleasant to be obliged to ford the river, which was often done, for at certain times the water ran so low that it could be done with safety. Mr. J. L. Begordis, of Peoria, resolved to build a ferry there. For this purpose he sent up a man, who built a shanty 8 by 10 on the bank, and lived there until Begordis sent up a carpenter to make the boat, who came a short time after. The carpenter, Mr. Doty, father of Mr. Elisha Doty of Polo, and his assistant, set vigorously at work, and it was not long until the boat was nearly half completed, when the Indians set fire to the boat, and informed them that they should not build a boat there, and told them to go to Peoria. This peremptory advice they concluded to accept with the best grace possible. Joe Ogie, a Frenchman, made the next attempt in the spring of 1828. He was an Indian interpreter, had married an indian woman, and was himself almost an Indian from his long association with them, having adopted many of their social and domestic habits. The red men were somewhat better pleased with him, and concluded to let him remain.

John Ankeney came from the southern part of Illinois in the spring of 1829, and made a claim at "*Nanusha*," or Buffalo Grove, by marking some trees on Buffalo Creek, near where the bridge on the "Galena Road" was afterwards built. He then returned for his family, and while he was gone Isaac Chambers came down from Galena with his family, and stopped at White Oak Grove—a small patch of timber lying about a half a mile west of the village of Foreston—where he remained only a short time. He was not exactly satisfied with this location, for he saw that in this country timber land must be more valuable than prairie, because of its scarcity. He therefore left that region and came ten

miles farther south to *Nanusha,* one of the largest groves in the whole country. He proceeded to make arrangements for building a house about thirty rods above the old bridge, where was a good place to cross the creek, and he had in contemplation a plan to change the line of travel from the prairie and have it pass through the grove, where he would build a "hotel" for the reception of travelers. While engaged in these preliminaries, he was surprised by the appearance of John Ankeny and family, who had come to take possession of his claim. Mr. Ankeney was no less surprised to find his claim had been taken by Mr. Chambers. The surprise was not exactly an agreeable one to either, although had either been so fortunate to have had entire possession it would have been a long way to his nearest neighbor. This consideration, however, was a matter of no consequence to them, and Mr. Ankeney, in no agreeable mood, went about a hundred rods farther down the stream, where he proceeded to erect a "Public House," although there was but one road in the whole country, and that one was two miles distant.

The hotels of the West in those days were not exactly of the same description as many we can boast of now-a-days. If they had any "up stairs," it was only accessible by means of the stones that projected from the rudely constructed chimney—which ran from the fire-place to the top of the house—or by pegs driven into the logs, and sometimes by a rough ladder made with an axe and pod auger. "Prairie bedsteads," too, were a prominent feature of the age. A sin-

5

34   HISTORY OF OGLE COUNTY.

Household Conveniences--Dividing Line between Ankeney and Chambers--Their Quarrels--Joe Ogle and his Squaw.

gle post was fastened to the floor, which was sometimes nothing more than the bare earth, without a carpet, about four feet from the wall; holes were bored into the logs of the side of the house, and sticks driven into the holes and fastened to the post, and then there were side rails running from the post each way, one to one side of the house and the other to the other side, slats placed crosswise for cords and the bedsteads were completed. These beds were often so made that by placing one above another, one "bed post" would support twelve sleepers. If the family consisted of both sexes, curtains of deer-skin or like material were hung between the beds, or else the light was put out just before retiring; this was done by covering up, or throwing water on the fire in the fire-place, which was the only light that could be afforded, for those were days of economy. Lights were found by striking flints and catching the sparks on tinder.

Having erected their houses, the next business before Mr. Ankeney and Mr. Chambers, was to survey the dividing line between them. The other boundaries need not be formally fixed, for, if they chose, the one could have Rock River on the one side and the other the Mississippi on the opposite side. One clear starlight night, when the moon did not shine, and when there were no clouds floating across the sky, they went out together to the south side of the grove, and from a red-oak stump they started towards the North Star, hacking the trees which stood in their way, the marked trees being the line between them.

All things being ready, they went to Ogle's Ferry, and staked out each his road, the two lines of stakes running parallel, being at no place more than half a mile apart. Chambers' stakes of course ran by his house, and Mr. Ankeney's by *his* house. The lines intersected north of the grove, and the main line, after continuing a considerable distance, again intersected with the old "Boles' Trail." No difficulty was found in inducing travelers to take one of the two proposed roads, but the question was, *which* road should they take? Each at once set at work to make his own house the most attractive. Jealousy and rivalry arose between them, and were harbored as long as they lived so near together with such conflicting interests. Each used every means in his power to injure the custom of the other, by such acts as felling trees across the other's road, in many other equally irritating ways, which rendered it quite an unpleasant neighborhood.

Meanwhile Ogle and his wife were not without their share of domestic difficulties. As they had no neighbors near enough to quarrel with, they managed to stir up a quarrel between themselves, which resulted in the separation of the family, and Joe was left to run his boat and broil his broth alone.

Mrs. Ogle owned nearly one half of Paw Paw Grove, which was an Indian reservation, consequently, after their separation, she was regarded as a *"rich widow,"* and as rich widows are personally attractive, it was not long before she found an admirer in the person of Job Alcott, whom she married, and this couple sub-

HISTORY OF OGLE COUNTY. 35

First Settlement at Dixon—Rates of Ferriage—Kellogg buys out Chambers—Settlements between Peoria and Galena.

sequently went to Kansas with her people, the Pottawatomies.

Early in 1828, a Mr. Clempson procured of the State Commissioners the contract for carrying the mail from Peoria to Galena, and he in turn gave the contract to Mr. John Dixon, from whom the town of Dixon took its name. Mr. Dixon's son commenced driving the stage early in the spring, before Ogie's ferry was in operation. He often experienced much difficulty in getting the Indians to ferry him over the river, and was sometimes exposed to much danger in attempting to swim his team. Ogie had been running the ferry nearly two years; his wife had forsaken him, and withal he was much disposed to change his course of life, when, on the 11th of April, 1830, Mr. Dixon came with his family from Peoria and bought out his ferry, &c., and took charge of it himself. The rates of ferriage were such as to make it a profitable business, for instance: For a yoke of oxen and wagon, 75 cents; for a span of horses and wagon, 75 cents; for a two-horse pleasure wagon, $1; for a horse and gig, 50 cents. The annual income of a ferry at these rates, when we consider the immense amount of travel, must have been very large.

At Burr Oak Grove, in the township of Erin, Stephenson county, Oliver W. Kellogg made a settlement in 1829. Here he remained until the spring following, when he removed to Buffalo Grove, where it seems Chambers was getting worsted in his competition with Ankeney, so that Kellogg and he were not long in making a trade. Chambers removed to a grove about six miles farther North, which became known as "Chambers' Grove." Kellogg moved into the house Chambers had occupied, and took up the old plan of hostilities with Ankeney.

One hour before the arrival of Mr. Kellogg at Buffalo Grove, Mr. Samuel Reed and family came. Mr. Reed proceeded to make a claim on the south side of the grove, where he lived until his death, which was in August of 1852. It was in May that Kellogg and Reed settled here. In June of the same year, Messrs. Bush and Brooky, from Kentucky, settled on the farm which is now owned by D. B. Moffat on the north side of the grove.

In those early days a road or track through the country was quite as important as the railroad is now—indeed they were far more scarce; so, the road from Peoria to Galena became well-known, and settlers took up their abode at convenient places along its line. In 1831, there was a settler at LaSalle prairie, about fifteen miles north of Peoria. John Boyd lived about twenty miles above La Salle Prairie, at what is now known as Boyd's Grove. A Frenchman, whose name was Bullbony, lived about eight miles farther north. Henry Thomas lived at the head of Bureau Timber, twelve miles from Boyd's Grove. The next settler was Joseph Smith, who lived at a grove which was called "Dad Joe's Grove" in honor of this early settler; this is nineteen miles south of Dixon. Dixon was the next, then Buffalo Grove. Mr. Crane, who afterwards moved to Crane's Grove, lived at Cherry Grove. Mr. John Flack

36   HISTORY OF OGLE COUNTY.

Settlements among the Indians—The Black Hawk War—Indian Treaties—Black Hawk's Pretences.

lived on Rush Creek, and the next settler north of Buck Creek was John Winters, on Apple River, where Elizabeth now stands. Mr. Winters afterwards moved to Buffalo Grove. North of Apple River, towards Galena, there were only two or three miners' huts. One of these belonged to William Durley, who was afterwards shot by the Indians in Buffalo Grove.

During this time, every settlement in the country had been made in the midst of Indians. The Winnebagoes had not yet left the country, and the Pottawatomies, who, however, were a smaller tribe, still lived on their old hunting-grounds. They were very peaceable, never even manifesting a disposition to pilfer or perform any of those little irritating acts which used to be so common with some Indians when they were in a state of professed peace.

CHAPTER X.

We come now to the Black Hawk War. Black Hawk himself was by birth one of the Sac tribe, being born on Rock River in 1767. The territory occupied by the Sacs at that time had originally been the property of the Sauteux (a branch of the Chippewa nation) and Iowas, and was wrested from them by the Sacs and Foxes, who came from Canada. By the treaty of 1804, (the provisions of which we have heretofore given,) these tribes ceded their lands to the United States. This treaty was confirmed at Portage des Sioux, September 13th, 1815,

by that portion of the tribes that had remained at peace with the United States during the war of 1812. The hostile part of the tribe (except Black Hawk and a few disaffected braves whom he called around him, all of whom professed to be British subjects, and went to Canada, where they received presents,) confirmed the latter treaty in the following year. Still further confirmation was given by another treaty made "with the chiefs, warriors and head men of the Sac and Fox tribes," at Fort Armstrong, (Rock Island,) on the 3d of September, 1822, in which the treaty of 1804 is referred to and ratified. On the 4th of August, 1824, a treaty was made at Washington, by which the Indians sold all their title to the northern portion of Missouri, from the Mississippi to the western boundary of the State, and the United States granted the strip of country between the Mississippi and Des Moines Rivers to certain half breeds of the nation, and on all the lands they had claimed *south and east* of the line, they were not to be permitted to settle or hunt after January 1st, 1826.

Black Hawk claimed that the chiefs who made the treaty of 1804 were made drunk while in St. Louis, (whither they had gone to procure the release of some of their nation who were in prison for murder,) and while intoxicated, they were induced to sell the lands of the tribe. Under this pretence that the treaty was void, he resisted the order for the removal of his tribe beyond the Mississippi. In the spring of 1831, Black Hawk and his party returned to their former principal village, to establish themselves on their ancient hunting grounds, and found that the government had surveyed and sold the land to settlers. He was accompanied in this expedition by some of the Pottawatomies and Kickapoos, and some three hundred warriors of the British band. The squaws proceeded to plant their corn as usual, which so annoyed the whites that they plowed up the land that had been planted. The Indians retaliated with annoyances which led the settlers to appeal to Gov. Reynolds for protection. The Governor construed Black Hawk's expedition into an invasion of the country, and forthwith wrote to Gen. Gaines of the United States Army, and to Gen. Clark, Superintendent of Indian Affairs, requesting them to do all they could to procure the peaceful removal of the Indians, but at all events to protect the settlers who had purchased lands. Gen. Gaines immediately repaired to Rock Island with a few companies of soldiers. Finding that the Indians were determined upon war, he called upon Governor Reynolds for seven hundred mounted volunteers. The Governor made a call upon some of the northern and central counties, and fifteen hundred volunteers rallied at Beardstown, and about the 10th of June were ready to march. On the 25th of the same month, the entire force reached Rock River, and the next day, when Gen. Gaines and his force entered the village, they found it deserted, the Indians having crossed the Mississippi the same morning. By the threats of Gen. Gaines to pursue them across the river, Black Hawk and the chiefs and braves of the band were led to sue for peace; and a treaty was here formed by which the band agreed to remain forever after on the west side of the river, unless permitted by the President or Governor to cross it. Thus Black Hawk and his party ratified the treaty of 1804, by which this region of country was sold to the whites.

Notwithstanding his treaty obligations, Black Hawk made his appearance in the Rock River country, in April, 1832, and prepared for war. He hoped to make the Winnebagoes and Pottawatomies his allies in this expedition against the whites; but in this he was disappointed. He reached the mouth of Rock River, and proceeded to ascend towards Prophetstown, the home of their prophet, Wabokieshiek, or "The White Cloud." The Indians were soon overtaken by an express from Gen. Atkinson, then at Fort Armstrong, ordering them to return to their homes on the west side of the Mississippi; but they paid no attention to these orders, and the party pressed on. Governor Reynolds, on learning of this new invasion, made another call for volunteers, which was responded to at Beardstown by about eighteen hundred men. The whole brigade was put under the command of Major General Samuel Whiteside, of the State militia. The first regiment was commanded by Col. Dewitt, the second by Col. Fry, the third by Col. Thomas, the fourth by Col. Thompson, and the spy battalion by Col. James D. Henry.

On the 21st of April, the army commenced its march, accompanied by Gov. Reynolds. On their arrival at the mouth of Rock River, Generals Whiteside and Atkinson agreed that the volunteers should march up the river to Prophets-town, and there await the arrival of the regular troops. Instead of waiting at that place, the men set fire to the village and marched to Dixon, where they came to a halt, and found two battalions of 275 mounted volunteers from the counties of McLean, Tazewell, Peoria and Fulton, under Majors Stillman and Bailey. As these officers begged to be put forward upon some dangerous service, they were sent up the river to spy out the Indians. Major Stillman left the main body of the army on the 12th of May, and on the 14th came to "Old Man's Run," now "Stillman's Run," a small stream which rises in White Rock Grove, in this county, and empties into Rock River near Byron. He encamped here just before night, and in a short time a party of Indians on horseback were discovered. Some of the party, without orders, mounted their horses and started in pursuit. They were joined by others. The Indians fled, but were overtaken, and three of them slain. Black Hawk and his main force chanced to be near by, and they soon rallied to the number of seven hundred men, and turned the pursuing volunteers back upon their own camp. The latter broke through the camp at full speed, throwing the entire force into confusion, spreading terror and dismay among the rest of the men, so that Major Stillman was unable to rally them. A retreat was commenced, and the whites scattered, straggling along in parties of four and five, until they reached Dixon.

Eleven of Stillman's men were killed, and under the circumstances we may well be astonished that the number was not greater.

The greatest consternation prevailed among the white settlements when the accounts of this action reached them. The reports, of course, greatly magnified the extent of the disaster, and made matters appear much worse than they really were. The settlers began to build forts and make preparations to defend themselves. Some families in the vicinity of the Indian camping ground were massacred before they could reach the forts.

In the night, after the arrival of Stillman's party at Dixon, General Whiteside called a council of war at his tent, at which it was agreed to march in the morning to the scene of the disaster. It was found that there were no provisions in the camp, except in the messes of some few of the men. Cattle and hogs, however, were obtained of Mr. John Dixon, who was the only white inhabitant on Rock River, so that in the morning the army were supplied with fresh beef, which they ate without bread. On their arrival at Stillman's Run, the volunteers found that the Indians were gone.

Intelligence of this engagement was immediately brought to Buffalo Grove, and the three families living there left for other places on the 15th—Mr. Samuel Reed's family going to Dixon, and Aukeney's and Chambers' (the latter living at Chambers' Grove,) going to Apple River Fort, now Elizabeth, while Mr. Kellogg's family went south.

Shooting of Durley at Buffalo Grove—Burial of the Dead at Stillman's Run—A new Army Raised.

On the morning of the 16th of May, an express party of six men left Galena for Dixon, consisting of John D. Winters, (now in California,) William Durley, Henry J. Morrison, Frederick Stahl, (now a prominent business man in Galena,) Charles R. Bennett and —— Smith. On arriving at Buffalo Grove, a consultation was held as to their best route through the timber. Their road lay through the north part of the grove, but some, who feared an attack by the Indians, advised that they should keep around the skirt of the wood, which made the distance a little greater, but was a route more likely to be safe. This advice was overruled, however, and the company proceeded directly on, when, just as they were entering the wood, the Indians fired upon them, and Durley was instantly killed. The rest wheeled their horses and made good their escape. Smith received a ball through his hat, just grazing the top of his head. Durley was buried on the very spot where he fell, and where his grave may still be seen. A little pine stands at the head of the grave; it still lives— a little shrub, as though it had just been placed there, for in ten years it has not grown an inch. The fence that was first placed around it became old and rotten and was fast falling to pieces, when about two years since it was replaced by another much prettier than the first, by the efforts of Mr. Squire Bruce, a resident of Buffalo Grove, who, by circulating a subscription, procured the means to rebuild it.

On the 21st of May, the Indians attacked Indian Creek settlement, fifteen miles from Ottawa, and killed fifteen persons, and took two young ladies, Silvia and Rachel Hall, prisoners, who were afterwards ransomed by Mr. Gratiot, through the Winnebagoes.

General Whiteside contented himself, on his arrival at Stillman's Run, with burying the dead, placing them in a common grave, on a ridge of land near the Run. He then returned to Dixon, where he met General Atkinson with the regulars. The army now numbered twenty-four hundred men; but the volunteers were anxious to be discharged. They were finally marched to Ottawa, where, at their urgent request, Governor Reynolds discharged them on the 27th and 28th of May.

Orders had been previously issued for raising two thousand volunteers, who were to meet at Beardstown and Hennepin. In the meantime a regiment was raised from the volunteers just discharged, and Jacob Fry was elected Colonel, James D. Henry Lieutenant Colonel, and Thomas Fry Major. General Whiteside volunteered as a private. The different companies of this regiment were so distributed as to protect all the frontiers. Captain Adam W. Snyder was appointed to guard the country between Rock River and Galena; and while he was encamped not far from Burr Oak Grove, on the night of the 17th of June, his company was fired upon by the Indians. The next morning he pursued them, four in number, and drove them into a sink hole, where his company charged on them and killed the whole of the Indians, with the loss of one man mortally wounded. As

40   HISTORY OF OGLE COUNTY.

Attack on Capt. Snyder's Party—Murder of St. Vrain—Attack on Apple River Fort—Bravery of the Women.

he returned to his camp, bearing the wounded soldier, the men suffering much from thirst, scattered in search of water, they were sharply attacked by about seventy Indians, who had been secretly watching their motions and awaiting a good opportunity." The men were taken by surprise and began a hasty retreat, when Capt. Snyder called upon General Whiteside for assistance in forming the men, who loudly declared that he would shoot the first man who attempted to run. The men were formed into rank, and both parties took position behind trees. Here General Whiteside shot the leader of the Indians, who then began to retreat. As they were never pursued, the Indians' loss was not known; the whites lost two men killed and one wounded."*

On the 15th of June, the new regiment arrived at the appointed places of rendezvous, and were formed into three brigades, under the command of Gens. Alexander Posey, Milton K. Alexander and James D. Henry. The whole volunteer force at this time amounted to three thousand two hundred men, besides three companies of rangers. Many of the Pottawatomies and Winnebagoes, though professedly at peace with the whites, were much disposed to join Black Hawk and his party, and it was hoped to overawe them by bringing so large a force into the field.

Before the new army could be brought into effective operation, several murders had been committed by the Indians. Among others, Mr. St. Vrain, the Indian Agent for the Sacs and Foxes, was murdered by a party under the lead of the

*Ford's History of Illinois.

chief "Little Bear," who had previously adopted him as a brother, and who treacherously murdered and scalped him and all but two of his party when they had confided themselves to his friendship.

In the latter part of the month of June, Black Hawk, with about one hundred and fifty warriors, planned an attack upon Apple River Fort. As they were lying in wait for an opportunity to make an attack, six men—Fred Dixon, formerly an Indian fighter in Missouri, Wm. Killpatrick, —— Walsh, —— Hackelrode and two others—carrying an express from Galena to Dixon passed them, and the Indian sentinel indiscreetly fired at them, wounding Walsh. Dixon immediately jumped his horse over Walsh as the latter lay upon the ground, and charged, single handed, upon the Indians, at the same time calling to his companions to carry Walsh into the fort. The Indians, supposing, from Dixon's movements, that the main body of the whites were close at hand, momentarily retreated, thus giving Dixon's companions an opportunity to retire to the fort, which they did, bearing Walsh with them. The alarm was thus given to the inhabitants in the vicinity, who rushed into the fort, which was immediately attacked by the whole of Black Hawk's troop. The fight lasted four or five hours, the whites bravely fighting to the last. The women in the fort displayed a coolness and courage worthy of the wives and daughters of the pioneers. They run bullets, loaded the guns and assisted the men by every means in their power. Hackelrode, one of the express party who escaped, was standing with his back toward one of the port-holes, while Mrs. Armstrong was picking the touch-hole of his gun, and an Indian fired at him and shot him in the back of the neck, killing him instantly. The whites finally succeeding in repulsing the Indians, who met with a heavy loss. Dixon's retreat to the fort having been cut off after his charge upon the Indians, he pressed on to Galena, where, however, the news preceded him, being borne there by Charles Bowers, who rode down the hill on the east side of Galena River, screaming, "Indians! Indians!" with all his might; and by the time that he had been ferried across, over an hundred people had collected on the levee to hear the news. Col. Strode commanded at Galena, and in the morning marched to the assistance of those in the fort, but did not arrive till the Indians had raised the siege and departed.

Having failed in this attempt, the Indians determined on their way back to secure a small guard of soldiers who had been left in charge of some military stores at Kellogg's house, in Burr Oak Grove. The guard had been removed before the Indians had reached the house, but Major John Dement (now a well known resident of Dixon) had shortly before come into the neighborhood with the Independent Spy Company attached to the first brigade, and with his company had encamped in Kellogg's house when the Indians reached there. Dement was not aware of the presence of the Indians till near morning, when the arrival of Captain Funk and a man named Duval placed him on his guard. Capt.

Funk's horse had a very great aversion to Indians, and would never remain in their presence. Captain Funk commanded at Scales Mound, and on receiving the news of the attack on Apple River Fort, he started in the direction of Burr Oak Grove with the hope of finding Dement. As the captain and Duval passed a thicket on the north side of the grove, the horse began to manifest the usual signs of the presence of Indians, and Funk was convinced that there were some lurking by. As soon as he found Dement, he told the latter his suspicions, and a small party of men were sent to reconnoitre, who soon returned and reported having seen a few Indians on horseback, who retreated on seeing them. When Dement's men heard that there were Indians about, they rushed out pell-mell, and began saddling their horses as best they could; and some of them came near being captured before they could get their horses, which were picketed at a considerable distance. Those who pushed forward to the attack upon the Indians were repulsed with considerable loss. When the whites returned to the house for shelter, the Indians commenced firing on the house, and at the horses which were fastened outside. Dement and Duval were standing in the door together, when two of the Indians came in sight, and before Duval could draw Dement's attention to them, they fired, one of the bullets whizzing by Duval's ear and lodging in the timbers of the house, while the other cut Dement's commission, which he carried in the crown of his hat.*

*History of Stephenson County.

Shortly after, two men mounted their horses and galloped to Buffalo Grove for reinforcements. As soon as they were out of reach, the Indians started for Rock River, doubtless guessing their object.

The whites lost five men in this action, and the Indians left three dead warriors behind them.

About the time of the attack on Apple River Fort, the Indians attacked three men near Fort Hamilton, in the Wisconsin lead mines, killing two of them, while the other escaped. Gen. Henry Dodge, who chanced to arrive at the fort soon after, in command of twenty men, started in pursuit, and chased the Indians to Horse Shoe Bend, on the Pecatonica, where they had taken shelter and were awaiting an attack from the whites. Gen. Dodge ordered his men to make a charge, and as they approached the place where the Indians lay, they were fired upon. Without giving them an opportunity to reload, the whites sprang upon the savages, some of whom tried to escape by swimming. Of the eleven Indians who formed the party, not one escaped. Four of the whites were severely wounded at the first fire, three of whom afterwards died from the effects of their wounds, and the other recovered.

About the 18th of June, a lot of horses had been stolen from Apple River Fort by the Indians, and Capt. James W. Stephenson, in honor of whom our sister county is named, started in pursuit of them. He surrounded them in a small thicket standing in the midst of a prairie, and made three successive charges upon them, but was finally compelled to retire with the loss of three men killed, and himself, with several others, severely wounded.

The Indians now held control of the country. Their war parties prowled about every white man's camp from Galena to Chicago, and from the Illinois river to the boundary of Wisconsin. They attacked every white man they came across, and, flushed with their victory, they were prepared for deeper and broader operations. But the position of matters soon changed. On the 20th, 21st and 22d of June, Gen. Atkinson took command of the forces assembled on the Illinois River, and put them in motion. Major Dement, with a battalion of spies, pushed forward and took position at Kellogg's Grove, in the heart of the Indian country. Hearing, on the 20th of June, that the trail of five hundred Indians leading to the south had been seen within a few miles the day before, Major Dement ordered his whole command to be in readiness, while he with twenty men started to gain intelligence of their movements. They had gone but a short distance when they discovered seven Indian spies. Followed soon after by some of the men from the camp, he formed about twenty-five of them in line to protect the retreat of those in pursuit. This had hardly been done when three hundred Indians came out to attack them. Seeing himself in great danger of being surrounded, the major slowly retired to his camp, closely followed by the savages. The whole party now took possession of some log houses, which served them for a

HISTORY OF OGLE COUNTY. 45

Movements of the Troops—Arrival at Lake Kuskanong—Progress of the Army- Difficulties of the Service.

fort, where they were vigorously attacked for nearly an hour, when the Indians retreated, leaving nine men dead on t e field, and probably five others carried away. The whites had five men killed and three wounded. An express had been sent to Gen. Posey, who arrived with his brigade about two, hours after the Indians had gone.

When the news of this action reached Dixon, where all the forces under Gen. Atkinson were assembled, Alexander's brigade was ordered in the direction of Plum river, to intercept the Indians if they attempted to escape by re-crossing the river. Gen. Atkinson, after waiting for two days at Dixon, marched up Rock River, accompanied by Gen. Henry's brigade. Col. Fry and his regiment were sent forward to meet some friendly Potta-watomies.

Black Hawk continued to move up the river, but finding himself closely pursued by the whites, he crossed over to the Wisconsin River. On the 21st of July, a detachment of troops *en route* for Fort Winnebago to procure supplies, discovered the Indians not far from Blue Mounds, and immediately attacked them, routing them and killing forty or fifty men. The whites had only one man killed and eight wounded.

Gen. Atkinson, having been informed that Black Hawk had fortified himself with his whole force at the four lakes, determined to decide the war by a general battle, and accordingly marched in that direction with as much haste as prudence would admit. On the 30th of June, he encamped at Turtle village, a town of the Winnebagoes, and encamped about a mile above it. He continued the march the next day, and on arriving at Lake Kuskanong was joined by Gen. Alexander's brigade. The country hereabout was thoroughly examined, and being convinced that there were no savages about, the General marched his whole force up the east side of Rock River, to Burnt Village, another Winnebago town, on Whitewater River, where he was joined by Gen. Posey's brigade and a battalion from Wisconsin under the command of Major Henry Dodge.

The progress of the army, up to this time, had been slow and uncertain. The country was almost an unexplored wilderness, and there was literally no reliable knowledge of the country among those composing the army, and the information to be gained from a few Winnebagoes who hung around the camp was delusive The frequent stoppages which were necessary in the midst of so much uncertainty only gave the savages opportunities to elude their pursuers.

Says Gov. Ford:

"Eight weeks now wasted away in fruitless search for the enemy, and the commanding general seemed farther from the attainment of his object than when the second requisition of troops was organized. At that time Posey and Alexander commanded each a thousand men, Henry took the field with twelve hundred and sixty-two, and the regular force under Col. Taylor, now Major General, amounted to four hundred and fifty more. But by this this time the volunteer force was reduced nearly one half. Many had entered the service for mere pastime, and a desire to participate in the excellent fun of an Indian campaign.

44   HISTORY OF OGLE COUNTY.

Destination of the several Brigades—Forced Marches—False Reports—Mutiny among the Troops.

looked upon as a frolic; and certainly but few volunteered with well-defined notions of the fatigues, delays and hardships of an Indian war in an unsettled and unknown country. The tedious marches, exposure to the weather, loss of horses, sickness, forced submission to command, and disgust at the unexpected hardships and privations of a soldier's life, produced rapid reductions in the numbers of every regiment. The great distance from the base of operations; the difficulties of transportation either by land or water, making it impossible at any time to have more than twelve days' provisions beforehand, still further curtailed the power of the commanding general. Such was the wastefulness of the volunteers, that they were frequently one or two days short of provisions before new supplies could be furnished.

"At this time there were not more than four days' rations in the hands of the commissary, the enemy might be weeks in advance; the volunteers were fast melting away, but the regular infantry had not lost a man. To counteract these difficulties, General Atkinson found it necessary to disperse his command, for the purpose of procuring supplies."

On the 10th of July, the several brigades were appointed to proceed to different destinations—Colonel Ewing's regiment being sent to Dixon as an escort for Capt. Dunn,* who was supposed to be mortally wounded; Gen. Posey marching to Fort Hamilton, (now Wyota, Wis.,) on the Pecatonica; and Henry, Alexander and Dodge being sent to Fort Winnebago, at the Portage, between the Fox and Wisconsin rivers; while Gen. Atkinson

* Capt. Dunn has since been elected a judge in Wisconsin, and in the campaign of 1858 was the Democratic candidate for Member of Congress, against Hon. C. C. Washburne, Republican.

himself fell back to Lake Kuskanong, where he built a fort and gave to it the name of the lake, and where he was to remain until the volunteer generals should return with supplies. Henry and Alexander reached Fort Winnebago in three days; Dodge preceded them a few hours by making a forced march. Two days were occupied in getting provisions, on the last of which the Winnebago chiefs present reported that Black Hawk and his forces were encamped at the Manitou Village, thirty-five miles above Gen. Atkinson, on Rock River. The commanding generals determined to violate their orders and march directly upon the enemy with the hope of taking him by surprise, or at least cutting off his further retreat to the north.

When they came to carry out this determination, Gen. Alexander's men mutinied and refused to go on the service, and soon infected Henry's men with the same spirit. All the officers of Col. Fry's regiment, except the Colonel himself, presented to Gen. Henry a written protest against the projected expedition. The only reply made by the General to this protest was to order the officers under arrest for mutiny, and to appoint Collins' regiment as a guard to escort them to Gen. Atkinson's camp. This had the effect to bring the protesting officers to terms; they humbly sued for pardon, and were profuse in their promises to return to their duty and never again to be guilty of like conduct. The General forgave them, and they returned to their posts.

On the 15th of July, Gen. Henry started from Fort Winnebago to search for the

Indians, accompanied by a half-breed named Poquette, and the "White Pawnee," a Winnebago chief, as guides. On reaching Rock River, he was informed that Black Hawk was encamped at Cranberry Lake, farther up the river. Relying upon this information, Gen. Henry determined to make a forced march in that direction the next morning.

"Doctor Merriman of Springfield, and W. W. Woodbridge of Wisconsin, were dispatched as expresses to General Atkinson. They were accompanied by a chief called Little Thunder, as guide; and having started about dark, and proceeded on their perilous route about eight miles to the southwest, they came upon the fresh main trail of the enemy, endeavoring to escape by way of the Four Lakes across the Wisconsin river. At the sight of the trail, the Indian guide was struck with terror, and without permission retreated back to the camp. Merriman and Woodbridge returned also, but not until Little Thunder had announced his discovery in the Indian tongue to his countrymen, who were in the very act of making their escape when they were stopped by Major Murray McConnell, and taken to the tent of Gen. Henry, to whom they confessed that they had come into the camp only to give false information, and favor the retreat of the Indians; and then, to make amends for their perfidy, and perhaps, as they were led to believe, avoid instant death, they disclosed all they knew of Black Hawk's movements."*

On the morning of the 19th, everything was in readiness at daylight for a forced march. Another express was sent to Gen. Atkinson, and all cumbrous baggage was thrown away. The sight of the broad fresh trail inspired every one with the hope that the war would soon be brought

to a close, and the men marched with better spirit than usual. In the afternoon of the first day, they were overtaken by one of those fearful storms so common on the prairie; but in spite of the pelting rain, the men pushed on, and during the day marched upwards of fifty miles, the officers in many instances dismounting and giving their horses to the men on foot. The storm continued until two o'clock in the morning, the men sleeping upon the muddy earth, covered with water. The rain prevented them building any fire to cook their food, and they made their supper and breakfast of some raw meat and some dough, formed by the flour in their knapsacks becoming drenched with the rain. The horses fared but little better than the men.

At daylight, on the 20th, the army was again on the march, and after as hard a march as the one of the day previous, they encamped on the banks of one of the four lakes forming the source of the Catfish River, in Wisconsin, and near where the Indians had encamped the previous night. They had now traveled one hundred miles without tasting any cooked food, and when they came to eat their suppers, it was probably with a relish they had never before known. They slept that night on the earth, with only the sky above them, and they slept soundly and well. The general expectation was that they would overtake the Indians the next morning, and all were in fine spirits. An alarm was giving during the night, by one of the sentinels firing at an Indian who was stealthily approaching the shore in his canoe. The whole

*Ford's History of Illinois.

46   HISTORY OF OGLE COUNTY.

The Pursuit Continued—Battle of Wisconsin Hights—The Volunteers joined by the Regulars at Blue Mounds.

force were at once under arms, but nothing more was discovered.

Early in the morning of the 21st, the march was continued as vigorously as before, the day's march being even harder than any which preceded it. About noon, the men in advance were close upon the rear-guard of the enemy, and the scouts ahead came suddenly upon two Indians and killed one of them as they were attempting to escape. By making false stands with a few warriors, as if to bring on a general battle, causing the whites to halt and make preparations to meet them, the Indians gained time to reach the bluffs on the Wisconsin River, by four o'clock in the afternoon. At this time, the advanced guard were fired upon by a body of Indians who had hidden themselves in the high grass. Major Ewing immediately dismounted his battalion and formed them in front, removing their horses to the rear. The Indians kept up their firing from behind the fallen timber.. Gen. Henry soon arrived with the main body, when the order of battle was immediately formed. Ewing's battalion and Jones' and Collins' regiments charged upon the Indians, who retreated before them and concentrated their force in front of Major Dodge's battalion. Col. Fry was sent to reinforce Dodge, and a general charge was now vigorously made along the whole line. The Indians stood their ground against Dodge and Fry and their men until they came within bayonet reach, when they fell back to the west and took a new position in the thick timber and tall grass in the head of a hollow leading to the river bottom. Ewing's battalion

and Collins' and Jones' regiments drove them from their new position and pursued them for some distance; but night coming on, further pursuit was stopped, and the troops slept upon the battle field. It was ascertained that the Indians left sixty-eight warriors dead upon the field, beside a large number wounded, many of whom were afterwards found dead on the trail. The loss of the whites amounted to one man killed and eight wounded.

Early next morning, the whites reached the Wisconsin River, and found that the Indians had crossed it and escaped to the mountains between the Wisconsin and the Mississippi. On account of the want of provisions, Gen. Henry determined to fall back to the Blue Mounds. They reached their destination in two days, where they met Gen. Atkinson with the regulars and Alexander's and Posey's brigades. After spending two days in preparation at the Mounds, the whole force, now under Gen. Atkinson's direction, again started in pursuit of the Indians. They crossed the Wisconsin at Wisconsin Hights, the scene of the late battle, (now Helena,) and struck the trail of the Indians among the mountains on the other side. The troops toiled sturdily in climbing the mountains and pushing through the deep swamps. The route was strewn with the bodies of the Indians who had died from the effect of wounds received at the late battle.

The misery of the Indians at this time was very great.* Their provisions had

*After giving an account of the battle at the Hights, Gov. Ford says: "That night, Henry's camp was disturbed by the voice of an Indian, loudly sounding from a distant hill, as if giv-

given out, and they were on the verge of starvation. They were so closely pursued by the whites that they could hardly find time to eat such food as they were able to procure. In addition to this, neglect and want of care of the wounds they had received brought disease, suffering and death among them to an almost incalculable extent, thinning their ranks with a fearful rapidity. A gentlemen who saw the Indians encamped at Rock Island, just after peace had been made with them, tells us that there was hardly a man, woman or child among them, whose bones did not almost protrude through the skin, so emaciated had they become!

On the morning of the fourth day after crossing the Wisconsin, the advance guard of Gen. Atkinson's army reached the east bank of the Mississippi, where the Indians had arrived some time before them. This was at Bad-Axe, about forty miles above Prairie du Chien. The steamboat *Warrior*, under the command of Captain Throckmorton, had descended to this point the day before, and prevented the

ing orders or desiring a conference. It afterwards appeared that this was the voice of an Indian chief, speaking in the Winnebago language, stating that the Indians had their squaws and families with them, and they were starving for provisions, and were not able to fight the white people; and that if they were permitted to pass peaceably over the Mississippi, they would do no more mischief. He spoke this in the Winnebago tongue, in hopes that some of that people were with General Henry, and would act as his interpreter. No Winnebagoes were present, they having run at the commencement of the action: and so his language was never explained until after the close of the war."

Indians crossing the river. In spite of a white flag raised by the Indians, Capt. Throckmorton fired upon them, killing twenty-three and wounding a great many more. Immediately after this affair, the boat dropped down to Prairie du Chien; and before its return the next morning, Gen. Atkinson had arrived with his forces and commenced a general battle.

Aware that the whites were in close pursuit of them, the Indians sent back a small party to meet the advancing troops within three or four miles of their camp, with instructions to retreat to a point three miles *above* their place of rendezvous—with the intent to draw the whites off the right trail. The ruse was successful, and Gen. Atkinson pursued the retreating party with the whole army, excepting Henry's brigade, which had been left in the rear. When Gen. Henry came to the place where the ruse had been played, he at once saw how the commanding general had been most egregiously deceived by the stratagem of the savage. By the advice of his officers, Gen. Henry was induced to march forward upon the main trail. He soon came up with the Indians, and a general battle commenced. The Indians were apparently taken by surprise, but they fought bravely and desperately, though without any plan or concert of action. Before Gen. Atkinson could arrive at the scene of action, the main work had been done. Henry had driven the Indians into the river, and his men were picking off the warriors who were trying to escape by swimming. A portion of the Indians had taken refuge on a small willow island near the shore, and were keeping up a severe fire upon the men on the shore. They were charged upon by some of the troops, and the most of them were either killed, captured or driven into the water, where they met a more certain death.

Many incidents are related as having occurred at the battle of Bad-Axe, which are of interest to the general reader. We have room for but one, which we find in a work upon the Black Hawk War, by Benj. Drake:

"A young squaw was standing in the grass, a short distance from the American line, holding her child, a little girl of four years old, in her arms. In this position, a ball struck the right arm of the child, just above the elbow, and shattering the bone, passed into the breast of its young mother, and instantly killed her. She fell upon the child and confined it to the ground. When the battle was nearly over, and the Indians had been driven to this point, Lieutenant Anderson of the United States Army, hearing the cries of the child, went to the spot, and taking it from under the dead mother, carried it to the place for surgical aid. The arm was amputated, and during the operation, the half starved child did not cry, but sat quietly eating a piece of hard biscuit. It was sent to Prairie des Chiens, and entirely recovered from its wound."

When the troops charged upon the Indians, the squaws and children were so closely commingled with the rest of the Indians that great slaughter took place among them, the squaws in many cases being dressed so nearly like the males that it was impossible to distinguish them.

The Indian loss in the battle of Bad-Axe was about one hundred and fifty killed, as many more drowned, and fifty prisoners taken. The Americans had seventeen men killed and twelve wounded.

With this battle ended the war. Black Hawk, who commanded in person the party whose movements had so deceived Gen. Atkinson, retreated to the Dalles on the Wisconsin river. A party of Sioux and Winnebagoes, headed by one-eyed Decori, a Winnebago chief, started in pursuit of them and captured them high up on the river. Among the prisoners were a son of Black Hawk and the Prophet, the latter being a noted chief who formerly lived at Prophetstown, Whiteside county, and who was one of the principal instigators of the war. The party were delivered to Gen. Street, the Indian agent, at Prairie du Chien.

The troops went down to Prairie du Chien, where they met Gen. Scott, who had been sent to take the chief command. On their route up the lakes, the troops under his command were afflicted with Asiatic cholera, which was then making its first appearance on the continent. In the course of a few weeks, nearly three hundred men had died from this disease. Gen. Scott reached Rock Island in August, but not until the war had been terminated by the battle of Bad-Axe.

On their arrival at Prairie du Chien, the volunteers were ordered to proceed to Dixon, where they were discharged. The men then proceeded to their homes

Black Hawk and his son, the Prophet and other head men, accompanied by many of the Winnebago chiefs, were sent to Rock Island, where a treaty meeting had been appointed; but on their arrival there, the cholera was so prevalent among

HISTORY OF OGLE COUNTY. 49

Treaty with Black Hawk and his Party—Black Hawk taken East—Gen. Atkinson—Tazewell and Jo Daviess Counties.

the troops that Gen. Scott and Governor Reynolds thought it advisable to drop down to Jefferson Barracks, where a treaty was formed by which the Sacs and Foxes " ceded to the United States a large tract of land bordering on the Mississippi, from the DesMoines to Turkey River, in the Territory of Iowa." For the faithful performance of the treaty, Black Hawk and his two sons, Wabokieshiek, Naopope and five other hostile Indians were held as hostages.

In the spring, the prisoners were taken East by order of the President, and after an interview at Washington, the prisoners were conducted through the Eastern cities, with the intention, on the part of the whites, of convincing them of the utter inutility of their efforts to drive the Americans out of the country. This had the desired effect. Black Hawk and Wabokieshiek professed a desire to live in peace with the whites. The party were at length taken to Fort Armstrong, where they were formally liberated, after giving many assurances of lasting friendship for the whites. Black Hawk remained steadfast to these promises during the rest of his life, and his lodge was at all times open to entertain his white visitors. He visited Washington again in 1837; but he was indifferent to all the attention shown him. He died on the 3d of October, 1840, at the age of eighty years, and was buried on the banks of the Mississippi.

The conduct of Gen. Atkinson in the Black Hawk War has been severely censured. We find an opinion prevalent among the early settlers, that he was dilatory in his movements at the beginning of the war, when prompt action would have suppressed the outbreak and ended the disturbances at once. His jealousy of the volunteers, as shown in his conduct after the battle of Wisconsin Hights, was in the highest degree discreditable to him as a man and a soldier. That he was in other respects a worthy man and a brave soldier, none will deny; and it is with regret that we mention the above facts.

CHAPTER XI.

We are now compelled to go back to supply some facts which were omitted in their proper order.

Previous to 1825, Tazewell county included the whole northern part of the State, extending for a considerable distance south of Peoria, which was then known as Fort Clark. On the 13th day of January, 1825, an act was passed, setting off Peoria county, which extended south of Peoria and north to the northern boundary of the State.

Jo Daviess county was formed by an act passed on the 17th of February, 1827, and included all the territory lying between the following boundaries: Beginning at the northwest corner of the State; thence, down the Mississippi River, to the northern boundary of the Military Tract; thence east, with said line, to the Illinois River; thence north, to the northern boundary of the State; thence west, with said boundary, to the place of beginning. By reference to the map, it will be seen that this includes at present a large num-

50   HISTORY OF OGLE. COUNTY.

Crossing Rock River in 1827—Bargaining with the Indians—The Darkey and the Red-Skins.

ber of the richest counties in the north-western part of the State.

Hon. J. Gillespie, of Edwardsville, has furnished us with the following interesting sketch of his experience in crossing Rock River at an early day:

"It was about the 5th day of March, 1827, that thirteen of us who had met together at different places and formed a traveling company for the lead mines, reached the banks of Rock River at the point, where, according to my recollection, Dixon now stands. It was naked prairie on the south side, but there was excellent hickory timber on the opposite side of the river. A band of Winnebagoes were encamped on the south side. It became necessary for a portion of our party to cross the river and prepare our encampment, and make fires in advance of the rest, and a Mr. Reed, my brother and myself were selected for that purpose. We had previously bargained with the Indians for the use of their canoes to ferry us and our wagon over, and had given a large amount of bacon and corn meal in payment. The Indians, without any reluctance, took Reed, my brother and myself across the river with our oxen, and as soon as we were separated from our companions, they started down the river with their canoes. This operation was likely to be attended with much inconvenience, and some suffering and exposure to us who had crossed the river and were without provisions or bed-clothes. Our friends followed down after the Indians, who pretended that they understood the contract on their part to have been fulfilled. We knew that they were endeavoring to fleece us. It was found impossible to bring them to agree to our understanding of the bargain, and nothing was left for our side but to make the best terms we could. They would not agree on any conditions we could propose, to ferry our wagon over, pretending to believe that it would sink their canoes. There was in our company a negro, named Frank, from Kaskaskia, who had

joined us when the company consisted of but four persons—old Mr. Reed, his son, my brother and myself; the rest of the company we picked up afterwards. We rather took care of Frank, and protected him when attempts were made to impose upon him, for which he was very grateful. Frank was in great distress when he found that three of his friends were separated from the company, and were without food or bed-clothes. He had a black overcoat, the body of which was about of the texture of an old sleazy blanket, but the capes were really of first rate material, and were fastened to the body with hooks and eyes. One of the Indians took a great liking to Frank's coat, and a bargain was struck on about these terms: Frank was to give the Indian his coat and they were to allow him to bring us over bed-clothing and food, and also to ferry the wagon over the next morning, upon terms to be agreed on. Frank rolled up an auger in the blanket to enable us to build a raft in case it should become necessary, but the Indians were too sharp for that. They unrolled the blanket and contended that taking over an auger was not in the bargain, and so Frank came over without it. When they arrived, a great controversy arose between him and the Indians. Frank contended that he was to give only his coat, and they contended that he was to give the cape also. We had by this time become so incensed at the Indians that we felt very little like obeying the scriptural requirement—'If any man will sue thee at the law and take away thy coat, let him have thy cloak also.' So we decided in Frank's favor, and he kept his capes. The Indians were very indignant at Frank's strict construction, and we might have had trouble with them; but that night it turned intensely cold, and by the next morning the Indians were as torpid as snakes in winter. They could not get out of their wigwams, and our men helped themselves to the canoes, and everything was pushed across early in the day. I believe the Indians would scarcely have aroused themselves if they had known that we were about massacreing them. I am satisfied that Indians suffer more from cold weather (clothed as they are) than white men. We experienced very little inconvenience from the cold.

"Lest what I have stated might lead persons to believe that all the Indians were thus knavishly inclined, I would remark that in crossing the Winnebago swamps some ten or fifteen miles south of Rock River, we had great difficulty, and would have had more but for some Winnebago Indians who were encamped by the swamps, and who were exceedingly kind and generous to us, and rendered us every assistance in their power.

"According to my recollection, there was a house about twelve miles northwest of Fort Clark, (now Peoria,) at which a man named Thomas Cox was lying very sick. We all called to see him, although not one of us was acquainted with him; but such was the custom (to some extent) in those days. This house was the last we saw until we reached Vinegar Hill, in the mines. The intervening country was one untrodden solitude. In most places the country was, even in that season of the year, of surpassing loveliness. Some of the groves reminded me of the description I have read of the fabled Elysium or of Mohammed's Paradise (save the Houris.) The only indications we found that human beings had been there before us, were where the Indians had cut off the branches of trees in which the honey-bees had made their hives. The groves seemed to have been almost alive with them, judging from the number of trees from which they had been dislodged. The Indians would not cut down the trees, but would climb up and cut off the limb which contained the honey, or cut into the side of the tree where the hive was in the trunk. I have observed that for a few years after the honey-bee makes its first appearance, it increases with wonderful rapidity, and after some ten or fifteen years, begins to decline. I am speaking now of the wild bees. They had been but for a few years in

the country between the Illinois and Rock rivers when I passed through. They had not arrived in the mining country until about 1826, or perhaps the spring of 1827. It is a fact perhaps not generally known that the honey-bee is just in advance of the white population in the settlement of a new country, and its first appearance is a cause of great anxiety to the Indians."*

We find that we were in error in stating that O. W. Kellogg and Samuel Reed arrived at Buffalo Grove in 1830. They settled here in 1831, one year later. In the spring of that year, the settlers broke the prairie and planted corn. The "first moon in June" was the time at which the Indians held their annual council; and when they met at Rock Island, it was rumored that they were going to make war upon the whites. Deeming it imprudent to remain here, the settlers started for Galena. On arriving at Apple River, their numbers were considerably increased by the addition of several persons from other points, and they concluded to stop and build a stockade. They had been here just a week, and commenced

*In a note accompanying the above sketch, Mr. Gillespie says: "In regard to the Winnebago Indians I would remark that from all I could learn they were regarded by the other tribes in the vicinity as intruders; that their language was entirely different from the surrounding Indians, and could not be acquired by them; that about the time I have spoken of, they were making their way rather eastwardly, until they were met by the white population coming West. Carver, an Englishman, who traveled through this country just before the era of our Independence, found them about Prairie du Chien, where they were governed by a Queen. They had a tradition at that time that they had come from west of the Rocky Mountains; that they had attacked a Spanish cavalcade, or train, loaded with white metal or silver, and killed the attendants, and were consequently driven off by the Spaniards. I mention these circumstances merely from memory, not having seen Carver's Travels since I was a boy, and so I may be somewhat mistaken as to what he says."

cutting the timbers for the fort, when a dispatch was received from Rock Island, informing them that a treaty had been made, and that they might safely return to their farms. On their return, the farms were fenced, in order to secure the growing crops. Before the crops could be harvested, provisions grew short, and the settlers were obliged to go to Peoria county for supplies.

When autumn came, the corn crop was light and late. After being harvested, the grain was grated on a grater, to get meal for bread, until it was too dry, when it was pounded in a mortar. The mortar was made by boring and burning the end of a log prepared for the purpose. The pestle was made by fastening an iron wedge to a "spring-stick" attached to an upright post, (much in the fashion of a well-sweep;) handles were then put on, when the operator commenced pounding, the elasticity of the stick lightening the labor by raising the wedge after it had struck the corn. This rude mill was generally used once a day. The Indians who were their nearest neighbors supplied them with venison during the winter, receiving corn and pumpkins for their compensation. The winter was long and tedious, with deep snows and high winds.

In April, 1832, the settlers commenced plowing. They had heard and seen that the Indians were going up Rock River, to plant corn, as they said. One day, some of their old Indian friends called upon Mr. Reed's family with some fresh fish, and one of them told the family that Gen. Whiteside was coming up the river with "heap Chemokee man," to fight the In-

dians. Said he, "You must go away—bad Indian kill you—me no kill you—bad Indian kill you and your papooses." Mr. Reed had planted his potatoes and about two acres of corn; this had been done on Saturday. On Sunday, there was a heavy fall of rain, which made it too wet for planting. On Monday evening, the report of firearms was heard in the direction of Kellogg's house, which, on account of the number of shots, greatly alarmed Mr. Reed's family. Gen. Dodge, with a scouting party, had encamped here, and had fired off their guns on arriving at Kellogg's house. The next morning, before sunrise, a messenger from Gen. Whiteside's camp arrived, with the news of the battle of Stillman's Run, and telling them that they must immediately go to Dixon, where the army was encamped. As soon as possible, their "traps" were loaded, and they started. After staying a few days in Dixon, Mr. Reed's family went to Peoria county with a company of volunteers who were going south to get their discharge. In September, the men returned to their farms, leaving the women and children in Peoria county. After plowing, sowing wheat and making hay, they returned and again brought their families to Buffalo Grove.

In 1833, it was rumored that the Indians were dissatisfied with the treaty they had made, and were bent on war. For the third time the citizens of Buffalo Grove left their homes, taking their families with them to Peoria county. The men immediately returned to cultivate the crops; and before harvest time came, the families were sent for. This was called "Mammy Dixon's War," from the fact that the alarm was caused by Mrs. Dixon's overhearing a conversation between some of the Indians, in which they expressed their dissatisfaction with the treaty. No outbreak occurred, however, and this was the last time the settlers at Buffalo Grove were driven from their homes by "wars and rumors of wars."

The first wedding ever celebrated in this vicinity was at the house of John Ankeny, early in 1832, when S. M. Journey was married to Ankeney's only daughter. All the neighbors (except Kellogg's family) for miles about were invited and were present on the joyous occasion; many persons from Galena, Rush Creek and the southern part of the State, were also there. The dancing and festivities were kept up till near morning, when the happy couple were put to bed in real old-fashioned style. Journey afterwards went to California, where he still remains, while his wife is living at Lyons, Iowa.

We may here remark that the first newspaper issued in Chicago was published on the 26th of November, 1833, under the title of *Chicago Democrat*, by John Calhoun. In 1836, John Wentworth purchased Mr. Calhoun's interest, and has continued to publish the *Democrat* from that time to this—an example of steadfastness rarely to be found in the history of Western newspaper enterprises. Mr. Calhoun died February 20th, 1859, in the 51st year of his age. For many years the settlers in this section depended almost entirely upon the *Democrat* for news

from the East; in fact, the *Democrat* and the Galena *Advertiser* were for years the only newspapers circulated in this region.

In 1834, Elisha Doty came from Peoria with his family, and settled at Buffalo Grove. In the same year, Ankeny removed to the farm now owned and occupied by Harry Smith. In May of that year, Albion Sanford and his family settled here, and in the fall they were followed by Cyrenus, Ahira and Harrison Sanford, with their families. Mr. Cyrenus Sanford was the father of Ahira, Albion and Harrison Sanford; he continued to reside at Buffalo Grove, on the same quarter section which he first " claimed " on his arrival here, until his death, which occurred on the 28th of May, 1858. In 1834, a Mr. Sackett became a resident of Buffalo Grove. Pearson Shoemaker, now a resident of Elkhorn Grove, near the Ogle and Carroll county, line settled here in the same year. On the 4th of September, 1834, Cyrus Doty, the first white native of Ogle or any of the adjoining counties, was born at Buffalo Grove, where he still resides, having now a family of his own.

The first school ever taught in this county was at O. W. Kellogg's house, in Buffalo Grove, in the winter of 1834-5, by Simon Fellows. In 1836, the building now occupied as a church by the United Brethren, at Buffalo Grove, was erected for the double purpose of a church and school-house—being the first building erected anywhere in this vicinity, for educational purposes. In the winter of 1836, there was a singing-school in this school-house. The building was built by subscription

54   HISTORY OF OGLE COUNTY.

Town of St. Marion (now Buffalo) Laid Out—First Saw-Mill—Wilson's Mill—Buffalo in 1837.

In 1835, the citizens of Buffalo Grove received several accessions to their numbers, among whom were John D. Stevenson, George Webster and the Waterburys, all of whom are now living in the vicinity. Previous to 1835, the inhabitants of the Grove were obliged to go to Dixon's Ferry for their mail matter. In the winter of that year, a Post-Office was established at the Grove and Elkanah P. Bush appointed Postmaster. At this time there was no Post-Office at Rockford. Bush did not remain in office for any length of time, but was soon removed and O. W. Kellogg appointed in his stead.

In 1835, O. W. Kellogg and Hugh Stevenson laid out what is now the town of Buffalo, and called it St. Marion. About this time, V. A. Bogue was the only lawyer in the county, and to him were referred all intricate questions of law, his judgment being considered final.

The first crop of winter wheat raised near Buffalo Grove was in 1834, from which time up to 1845, very little spring wheat was grown.

The first saw-mill erected in Ogle county was the one now owned by John D. Stevenson, at Buffalo Grove. This mill was built in 1836, the proprietors being O. W. Kellogg, George D. Wilcoxen and Reason Wilcoxen.

Up to 1838, almost the only money in circulation, was of the "red-dog" stripe. Good money was very scarce, but these pictured "promises to pay" were very abundant in proportion to the scarcity of gold and silver. The harvests were abundant, but there was no market, ex-cept in the lead mines. Cash had to be paid for sugar—wheat not being considered equivalent to it.

It may be interesting to note here that the only member of O. W. Kellogg's family now living, is his daughter, the wife of E. B. Baker, Postmaster at Dixon. Mr. Kellogg became involved and lost his property, and, as a matter of course, his friends deserted him when his misfortune overtook him. He afterwards became a Minister of the Gospel, and died in Dixon. His wife, who was in every way a superior woman, survived him only two or three years.

"Wilson's Mill" was begun in 1835 by Joseph M. Wilson and James Talbot, and commenced grinding corn in June 1836. Wheat was ground there in the fall of the same year. Phelps' saw-mill on Pine Creek was running in 1836; it is still in operation.

C. G. Holbrook, Esq., says: "When we came from Dixon in 1837, and came up on the rising ground three miles north of that place, there was not a single foot of ground to be seen which the hand of man had touched. Men were located in the country, but were in the hollows and groves where they could not be seen." Since settlements have been made, many of the prairie flowers have disappeared, being destroyed by the cattle and the fires. When settlers first arrived here, there was no underbrush in the groves, as the spring fires always kept it down, and one could see almost as far in the groves as in the prairies.

Lawsuits were commenced in 1836 and continued until 1839, growing out of the

HISTORY OF OGLE COUNTY. 55

First Settlement at Oregon—Organization of Ogle County—Seat of Justice at Dixon—First Election.

original claims of Ankeney and Chambers in Buffalo Grove. How the suits were decided is a matter of no particular importance to our readers, but it is interesting to notice the perpetuation of the quarrel.

J. W. Jenkins, in 1835, built the first house in the present town of Oregon. In the year preceding, Martin C. Hills, Jehiel Day and a Mr. Goodwin made a claim on the prairie bordering on the river, and adjoining the village of Oregon, on the south. In 1835, John Phelps, now living in Texas, settled on his farm a short distance from Oregon, and shortly after, in company with some others, laid out that town. Thomas Ford, afterwards Governor of the State, arrived in 1836, and was soon followed by W. W. Fuller, James V. and John Gale; the latter two are now the oldest settlers residing in the place. The first school in Oregon was taught by a Mr. Whitney, in 1839. In 1836, there were no settlements on the East side of the river from Oregon to Inlet. In that season, however, a piece of ground was broken near Washington Grove by a Mr. Stevenson, another near Oregon by William J. Mix. The country on the west side of the river was being more rapidly settled.

At the session of the Legislature held in 1835-6, Ogle county was organized, and embraced the territory now included in the three counties of Ogle, Lee and Whiteside. The county seat was located at Dixon, and the first Circuit Court convened there in October, 1837, Hon. Daniel Stone, Judge, presiding. William W. Mudd was Sheriff, and William J. Mix was his Deputy. Smith Gilbraith,

of Dixon, was Clerk, and Thomas Ford, Prosecuting Attorney. The name Ogle was given in honor of Capt. Ogle, at the suggestion of Gov. Ford. During his lifetime, Capt. Ogle was a resident of the southern part of the State. Among the jurors chosen at the first Circuit Court, will be found many familiar names. Among the Grand Jurors were John Whitaker, Lester Evarts, William Wamsley and G. D. H. Wilcoxen; and among the Petit Jurors we find E. Kimball, Jared Sanford, James V. Gale, Elisha Doty and John D. Stevenson.

The first election in Ogle county of which we have any record was held at Oregon on the 24th day of December, 1836. The following is the record, as we find it in the County Clerk's office:

"At an election held at the house of John Phelps in Oregon City, in the County of Ogle, and State of Illinois, on the 24th day of December, 1836, the following named persons received the number of votes annexed to their respective names for the following described offices, to wit:

Isaac Rosecrans, for County Commissioner			89
Ezra Bond, " " "			90
Wm. J. Mix, " " "			87
Cyrus Chamberlain, " " "			95
S. St. John Mix, " " "			98
V. A. Bogue, " " "			98
Wm. W. Mudd, for Sheriff			95
Jeremiah Murphy, for Sheriff			98
Lester H. Evarts, for Coroner			94
James V. Gale, for Recorder			138
B. T. Phelps, for Recorder			48
Joseph Crawford, for Surveyor			119
Wm. Sanderson, for Surveyor			63

Certified by

JAMES V. GALE,
G. W. ROSECRANS,
JONATHAN W. JENKINS,
Judges of Election.

GEORGE CHANDLER,
SMITH GILBRAITH,
Clerks of Election.

It is related that a party of voters from

Guffalo Grove lost their way on their return from attending the above election, while in the region of Pine Creek, and did not reach their homes till several hours after their companions, who had preceded them.

At this time, instead of the present township organization system, the county affairs were principally administered by a Board of Commissioners. The first Board chosen consisted of V. A. Bogue, (now our County Judge,) S. St. John Mix and Cyrus Chamberlain. The first County Court was held by Commissioners Bogue and Mix, at Oregon, on the 3d of January, 1837, Smith Gilbraith being Clerk. The second term of this Court was held at the house of F. Cushman, in Buffalo Grove, in the following March. At this sitting of the Court, the county was divided into election precincts as follows: Bloomingville, (now Byron,) Oregon City, Grand Detour, Buffalo Grove, Dixon and Inlet.

A petition was presented by L. Andrus and others, asking for the appointment of viewers to locate a road from Dixon's Ferry to Grand Detour; thence to Oregon, on the west side of the river; thence to Bloomingville. The petition was granted and the present road was laid out shortly after. A license was also granted for establishing a ferry at Grand Detour.

The town of Byron, which was early called Bloomingville, was first settled in 1835. Jared Sanford came from the "Military Tract" in the month of June, in that year. On arriving at Rockford, by his pleasant story of the country through which he had passed, and especially of a mill site he had found near where Byron is now situated, he induced Perry Norton and James Sanford to return with him. They, being as well pleased with the country as he was, laid claim to all the country in the vicinity, according to the custom of those times. Mr. Norton is a native of New-York, and at the time of which we are now writing had been visiting his brother at Galena, where he "hired out" to Germanicus Kent, and had gone to Midway, by which name Rockford was then known, to perform the work he had been hired to do. Mr. Norton, in company with several other young men who were at work with him, came to Midway in the previous fall, where they kept "bachelor's hall" during the winter. In the spring, Mr. Mr. Norton's family, which was the first, came to Midway. At the time that Messrs. Norton and Sanford left Rockford, there were but two families there. In the fall of '35, P. J. Kimball and M. M. York settled at Byron, and in the spring of '36 came S. O'Brian, Asa Spalding, Simon Spalding and James Spalding. The family of Mr. Shepherd was the first to come to Fairview, as the place was called before the name was changed to Bloomingville. In the winter of '36-7, a number of families, including those of Erastus Norton, S. St. John Mix and Lucius Reed, settled in the place. The first school-house in the place was built during this winter, and we believe the first school was taught in the summer following.

After the organization of Ogle county

HISTORY OF OGLE COUNTY. 57

Division of the County—Regular Preaching of the Gospel—Gangs of Desperadoes in the Country.

in 1836, a great deal of excitement and strife ensued in regard to the county seat. The first Commissioners were favorable to Dixon, and held their sessions there. In 1838, the Oregon party succeeded in electing their candidates, and the county business was at once transferred to Oregon. The Commissioners soon made a contract for building a court house, and thus *fixed* the county seat. As soon as this was done, the people of Dixon commenced agitating the question of a division of the county. John Dixon had posted, in Galena, notices of his intention to apply for the formation of a new county—the proposed territory including Oregon on the north. John Phelps, of Oregon, chanced to be in Galena and discovered the notices which Dixon had posted, and he immediately posted like notices of *his* intention to apply for a division of the county, the southern line of his county just including the present town of Dixon. Learning this fact, and being fully aware that if Mr. Phelps' project was successful, it would greatly detract from the importance of his town, Mr. Dixon at once called upon Mr. Phelps, when a compromise was agreed upon and the present limits of the two counties were fixed, and a joint petition was sent to the Legislature, the prayer of which was granted. The act for the separate organization of Ogle and Lee counties, is dated February 27th, 1839. Horatio Wales, now residing at Buffalo Grove, was the first Sheriff after the new organization. In the spring of 1839, the first Circuit Court was held at Oregon, Judge Ford presiding.

We find in the Mt. Morris *Gazette* of July 17, 1851, a statement that the first *regular* preaching of the Gospel in this region was in 1834–5, by Rev. Mr. Sugg, a young Methodist missionary, who here began his ministerial labors. Before he had spent a single year in his Master's service, he was called to his reward. In 1835, Rev. James M. Kean was sent into this field by the Conference. Mr. Kean died at Elkhorn Grove about two years ago.

S. M. Bowman was the first man who ever lectured on Temperance in Dixon. It was at a Fourth of July celebration at an early day.

CHAPTER XII.

From 1835, for many years following, the northern part of the State was infested by numerous bands of desperadoes, whose principal business was robbery, horse-stealing and counterfeiting. Many of them "ranged" through Ogle and the adjoining counties. Among the most notorious in this section were William K. Bridge, the leader of the gang, Norton B. Royce, ——— Driskell, William Driskell, Taylor Driskell, Charles Aiken, Richard Aiken, ——— Broady and Hugh Broady; Broady's Grove took its name from the Broadys. The depredations of this gang troubled the settlers to a great extent. So frequently were their lawless acts committed, that there was no security for property of any kind. About the year 1840, the desperadoes were so numerous as to be able to control elections in this, county, and often procured some of their own number to sit on juries, by which means they were acquitted of all charges.

In the summer of 1840, a court house was built, and the people were congratulating themselves upon having a proper building for holding Courts. They had long been harassed by the gang of villains who rendezvoused at Washington Grove, and they hoped that the new facilities they now had would aid them in bringing the scoundrels to justice. In this, however, they were disappointed, the depredations proving more frequent and being more boldly carried out. At last, finding the law powerless in their defence, the people formed a band of Regulators, with the avowed intention of taking the law into their own hands. The Regulators were commanded by a Mr. Campbell, a fugitive Canadian patriot, who was universally esteemed by his neighbors as a man of sterling character.

The court house erected in Oregon was never occupied for the sittings of Court. On the night previous to the opening of the Court, the court house was fired by the desperadoes, in the hope of being able, during the excitement of the fire, to liberate some of their confederates who were confined in jail. In this they were frustrated, although they succeeded in knocking the jailor down. Assistance was promptly at hand, and the prisoners were safely removed.

Previous to the formation of the band of Regulators, Norton B. Royce had been convicted of counterfeiting and sentenced to the Penitentiary. Judge Ford presided during the trial, and after the prisoner had been sentenced, Judge Ford remarked that he was then going away on business, and should be obliged to leave his family behind him; and should the desperadoes dare to injure his family or property during his absence, he would follow them until he overtook them, when the first tree should be their gallows; and if the injury should be done while he was trying any case, he would leave the bench and follow them up till they were exterminated. Such language as this, from a judge on the bench, assured the people that Regulators had nothing to fear in a Court presided over by him; and this eventually led to the formation of the Regulators.

A man named Daggett had been horsewhipped at Payne's Point in the spring of 1841, and the notorious Bridge and some others, obtained of Esq. Wood a warrant for those who inflicted the punishment. The Sheriff being absent, the warrant was placed in the hands of Coroner James Clark, who, however, did not succeed in serving it—and so the affair ended.

One Daniel Ross was taken by the Regulators and made to hold on to the limb of a tree just high enough to allow his toes to rest upon the ground. Whenever he attempted to let himself down, the prompt and vigorous application of the cow-hide on his seat of honor, compelled him to take the old position.

These extreme measures of course aroused the most bitter feelings among the horse thieves and their associates, and they at once resolved to be revenged. One Sunday, as Capt. Campbell and his family

HISTORY OF OGLE COUNTY. 59

Murder of Mr. Campbell—Trial and Execution of the Driskells—The Rock River Register, the First Newspaper.

were passing from the gate to the house door they chanced to look about, and saw two men not very far from them. As they discovered the men, one of the latter drew up his rifle and shot Mr. Campbell through the heart, killing him instantly. Mr. Campbell's son—a "chunk of a boy," as he is described to us—ran into the house for his father's rifle, and bringing it out fired at the men, but they were out of reach and escaped.

This outrage, connected with others which had been committed by the gang, roused the citizens to more vigorous measures in self-defence. Old man Driskell and his son William were suspected of the murder and were at once arrested and taken to Oregon. The Regulators soon assembled *en masse* at Stevenson's Mill, on the creek running through Washington and Lafayette Groves, and proceeded to try the culprit. A temporary court was organized, counsel was granted the prisoners, witnesses were examined and cross-examined, and as fair a trial awarded them as could be given under the circumstances. It was decided that they must be immediately executed. A number of men with rifles were detailed to carry the sentence into execution. One of the prisoners was led out and shot, and then the other was led out, and after being shown the body of his dead relative, he was exhorted to confess that he had committed the crime charged against him. This he refused to do, but acknowledged that he had committed other crimes for which he deserved death.

The friends of the Driskells afterwards procured a bill of indictment against the Regulators, charging them with murder. The Regulators and their friends at once procured similar bills against every person who was present at the execution, the whole numbering about one hundred and twenty-five men; and as all were under indictment, it was impossible to find any witnesses, and all were cleared.

The remedy adopted by the citizens was a terrible one, but we cannot now call in question its wisdom. We must reflect, in judging of this matter, that the desperadoes were the most numerous, and were able to control the elections, thereby placing their own friends in power and confiding to them the execution of laws intended as a defence against their lawlessness. It was apparently the *only* remedy, and the early settlers showed much courage in making use of it.

CHAPTER XIII.

The first newspaper in this county was the *Rock River Register*, the first No. of which was issued in Mt. Morris on the first day of January, 1842, by Jonathan Knodle. We find in the first column of No. three, the earliest copy within our reach, the following:

TERMS,

Provided 400 subscribers be obtained:

The *Rock River Register* will be neatly and tastefully printed on a super-royal sheet of good quality, and published weekly at $2.50, in *advance*, per annum, or $3, if not paid in *advance*. $1.50, in *advance*, for six months;—otherwise no subscription will be received for less than a year.

60   HISTORY OF OGLE COUNTY.

First Wedding in Mt. Morris—Advertisements in the Register—Boundary Meeting at Oregon.

TERMS,

Provided 600 subscribers be obtained:

$2, in *advance;*—$2.50 in *postponement.*

$1, in *advance,* for six months.

☞ No paper discontinued until all arrearages are paid, but at the option of the publisher.

It was a small five-column sheet, printed on paper of a very inferior quality. The early numbers contains a Thermometrical Register, an Almanac, Market Reports from Baltimore, Cincinnati, Chicago and New-Orleans. In No. four we find the following:

MARRIED.—In this place on Sunday, Jan. 2, by the Rev. S. S. Walker, *Michael Chesire,* to *Margeret McAllister.*

[*There, that,* January 2, A. D. 1842, *is the Mt. Morris* NUPTIAL EPOCH *This is the first case of Matrimony which has ever occurred in Mt. Morris.*]

We also find the business cards of Henry Roberts and H. A. Mix, Attorneys at Law at Oregon; James J. Batty, Physician and Surgeon, at Mt. Morris; a dun from S. Cumins, and from the same gentleman a notice that he has removed to his new brick store, and has just received a larger and better stock of goods than is found within fifty miles of him; an advertisement of a stray bull from Henry Sharer; one of a stray heifer from Nathaniel Swingley; an administrator's notice in the matter of the estate of Wm. Driskell; an advertisement of boots and shoes from O. F. Palmer; a notice that D. Brayton & Son have have opened in Mt. Morris a large stock of everything usually kept in a country store; one that Miss Shepherd will give instructions in drawing and ornamental needlework; a few legal notices and newspaper propectuses, and at last the following announcement:

BOOKS,
WRITING PAPER,
QUILLS, PENCILS, WAFERS,
Blue and Black Writing Ink, and Inkstands,
Percussion Caps, Matches,
&c. &c. ALSO,—
A L M A N A C S
For 1842.
FOR SALE AT THIS OFFICE.
January 1, 1842.

The "motto" of the *Register* was credited to Rev. T. S. Hitt, and reads, "We hope to be recognized as fellow-laborers in the noble work of enlightening the human mind."

No. 3 of the *Register* for January 15, 1842, contains a call for a meeting on the Boundary Question, to be held at Oregon, on the 22d of that month. A subsequent issue contains a report of the proceedings of the meeting, which, as a matter for reference, we copy here:

"At a general meeting of the citizens of the county of Ogle and others, convened by public notice at Oregon City, on the 22d January, inst., for the purpose of considering the expediency of advising and effecting a separation of this section of the State from the State of Illinois and annexing the same to Wisconsin.

"The meeting was organized by the appointment of Col. D. Brown as Chairman, and Joseph B. Henshaw as Secretary.

"The following gentlemen were then appointed a committee to draft resolutions expressive of the sentiments of the meeting, viz: S. N. Sample, E. A. Hurd, D. T. Moss, W. W. Fuller and J. Swan, who retired for that purpose.

"A central committee of three were elected

to correspond with other committees and persons on all subjects of this meeting, with power to appoint precinct committees. The following gentlemen were elected to compose the central committee, viz: James V. Gale, Joseph B. Henshaw and E. S. Leland.

"The central committee appointed the following gentlemen correspondents of their respective precincts:

"Oregon Precinct—The Central Committee.

"Bloomingville—H. Norton and A. Wilbur.

"Maryland—N. Swingley and C. Marshall.

"Buffalo Grove—J. D. Stevenson and H. Wales.

"Grand Detour—S. Cumins and B. Butterfield.

"Washington Grove—J. Day and C. Rice.

"Brooklyn—D. Reed and R. Young.

"Monroe—H. Hill and I. Shearer.

"The committee appointed to draft resolutions returned and reported the following:

"WHEREAS, By an ordinance entitled 'an ordinance for the government of the Northwestern Territory,' it was ordained and declared by the Congress of the United States that there should be formed in the Northwestern Territory not less than three nor more than five States; and that in pursuance of said ordinance the States of Ohio, Indiana and Illinois were formed; And Whereas, it was also ordained and declared by the ordinance aforesaid, that the boundaries of those States should be subject so far to be altered that if Congress should find it expedient, they shall have authority to form one or two States on that part of the said Territory which lies north of an east and west line drawn through the southerly bend or extremity of Lake Michigan;' And Whereas, by virtue of the last mentioned power the State of Michigan and the Territory of Wisconsin have been formed north of said line; And Whereas, it is ordained and declared by the ordinance aforesaid, that the fifth article thereof; (that which defines the boundaries,) shall be considered one of the articles of compact between the original States and the people and

States in the said territory, and forever to remain unalterable, unless by common consent.

"Therefore Resolved, That in the opinion of this meeting that that part of the Northwest Territory which lies north of an 'east and west line through the southerly bend or extreme of Lake Michigan' belongs to and of right ought to be a part of the State or States which have been or may be formed north of said line.

"2d. Resolved, That Congress has established by said ordinance the southern boundary of the State which may be formed north of the State of Illinois, and that line cannot be altered without the consent as well of the original States as the people in the said Northwest Territory.

"3d. Resolved, That as part of the people of the said Northwest Territory, we will not consent to an alteration of said line so as to place us under the jurisdiction of a State to which we do not lawfully belong.

"4th. Resolved, That the lines as originally established by Congress in the 'ordinance for the government of the Northwestern Territory' are better suited to the geographical situation, and to the local interests of the said Territory than any others which can now be made.

"5th. Resolved, That we are decidedly opposed to alter the lines as originally established so as to place any of the territory north of the 'line drawn through the southern extreme of Lake Michigan' within the jurisdiction of a State south of said line, without the consent of the people of the said Northwest Territory.

"6th. Resolved, That it is expedient for the people now included in the State and residing north of a 'line drawn through the southerly extreme of Lake Michigan' to claim to be included in a State to be formed from the territory north of said line.

"7th. Resolved, That it be recommended to the Legislature of Wisconsin to apply during the present session of Congress to be admitted into the Union, claiming as a southern boundary of the State 'a line drawn through the southerly bend or extreme end of Lake Michigan,' and running due west to the Mississippi.

"8th. *Resolved,* That the liberal appropriation of the Legislature of the State of Illinois for internal improvements within our district embracing that part of the Northwest Territory claimed by Illinois was made in good faith, and that we disclaim any intention to absolve ourselves from any pecuniary responsibility created by the Legislature of Illinois for such purposes and hold sacred the legal obligations of the State.

"9th. *Resolved,* That a committee of nine persons be appointed as delegates from this county to proceed to Madison in the Territory of Wisconsin, with full power to consult with the Governor and Legislature, or either of them, of said Territory, and to take such measures as in their opinion will most speedily and effectually obtain the object of this meeting.

"The resolutions having been read, were fully debated, and respectively adopted unanimously.

"Agreeably to the 9th resolve, a committee was appointed to nominate nine delegates to the Governor and Legislature of Wisconsin or either of them, who having retired for that purpose returned with the following nominations, viz: W. W. Fuller, Dauphin Brown, Joseph B. Henshaw, Jehiel Day, James Swan, Spooner Ruggles, Samuel M. Hitt, Henry Hiestand, Augustis Austin.

"The above nomination having been submitted to the meeting, they were unanimously elected as delegates with power to fill any vacancies that may occur in their number.

"It was unanimously voted that the proceedings of this meeting be signed by the Chairman and Secretary, and published in the *Chicago American* and *Democrat, Galena Gazette, Rock River Register, Rockford Pilot,* and the Madison, Wisconsin, papers.

"DAUPHIN BROWN, *Ch'm.*
"JOSEPH B. HENSHAW, *Sec'y.*

"Oregon City, Jan. 22, 1842."

No. 6 of the *Register* speaks of the *Rockford Pilot,* twenty miles up the river, as its nearest newspaper neighbor. The same paper publishes the proceedings of a meeting held at Oregon on the 22d of January, 1842, for the purpose of forming an "Ogle County Agricultural Society." Spooner Ruggles was Chairman of the meeting, and D. H. T. Moss was Secretary. A constitution was adopted, H. Norton, Dr. A. Hurd and James B. Henshaw being the committee who drafted the document. In this issue are given some remarks made by Rev. T. S. Hitt, at the consecration of Mt. Morris Cemetery, February 2, 1842, and a list of the letters remaining in the Post-Office at Mt. Morris, January 31, 1842, signed by John Sharp, P. M. This list contains thirteen names!

In the *Register* of February 26th, 1842, is a notice signed "Many Citizens," to the effect that a petition would be presented to the Legislature for a division of the county by Rock River, north and south.

The same paper contains the proceedings of a meeting of the citizens of Stephenson county, at McDowell & Stoneman's, in Freeport, on the 19th of the same month, "for the purpose of considering upon the best measures to be adopted by the inhabitants on what is commonly called the 'disputed territory,' for the assertion and maintenance of the rights guaranteed to them by the ordinance of 1787. The meeting was called to order by O. W. Brewster, Esq., and on his motion, Maj. John Howe was chosen Chairman, and George Reitzell, Secretary.'

HISTORY OF OGLE COUNTY. 63

Report of the Delegates sent to Wisconsin—Removal of the Register to Grand Detour—Grand Detour in 1842.

This meeting was addressed by M. P. Sweet and O. H. Wright, and passed a resolution recommending that an election be held on the 5th of March, to decide whether or not the people in the proposed territory were desirous of forming an independent State. Judges of election were appointed for the several precincts, who were to make returns to the County Central Committee.

The question of boundary agitated the people of this section for many years, entering into their political conflicts and exercising an important influence. Many of the old settlers, to this day, condemn the act which fixed the present boundary line. The grounds of complaint are pretty well set forth in the preamble and resolutions adopted at Oregon.

On the 26th of February, another meeting was held at Oregon, to hear the report of the Committee sent to Wisconsin to confer with the authorities of that Territory. The Committee reported that they had received assurances of the earnest co-operation of Gov. Doty and the Legislature, who recommended that a census of the several counties in the "disputed territory" be taken, with a view to the presentation of a petition to Congress for the formation of a new State.

Subsequent issues give reports of "Boundary Meetings" in various parts of Northern Illinois, showing the feeling to be deep and wide-spread.

No. 12 of the *Register* bears the names of Knodle & Stephens as publishers, and announces the death of the Editor, Emanuel Knodle, in the 32d year of his age.

On the 10th of July, the *Register*

abandoned its neutral position and hoisted the Whig flag, headed with the name of Joseph Duncan for Governor, in opposition to Thomas Ford, the Democratic candidate, and denounced Judge Ford as "a Northern man with Southern principles," inasmuch as he was opposed to removing the northern boundary of Illinois.

The issue for September 16 is dated at Grand Detour, to which place it was removed on account of the mail arrangements—the mail at Mt. Morris "being reduced to a *weekly horseback*."

On the 7th of October, the paper was dressed in mourning, on account of the death of D. C. Dunbar, its Editor, aged twenty-eight years.

In the issue for October 14, the Editor writes of "Our Village," (Grand Detour.) After boasting of the healthiness of the place and the energy of its citizens, he says:

"We have two stores, one of which has sold upwards of thirty thousand dollars' worth of goods the past season, and furnished a market for a large quantity of wheat, pork and other produce, and a third to be filled in two weeks. One *good* hotel; two blacksmith shops; one plow factory, tin shop, cigar factory, one painter and glazier, two coopers and two carpenter shops, two shoemakers, cabinet shop, broom factory, one wheelwright and wagonmaker's shop, one turning shop for both wood and iron, one tailor, one physician, &c.; one grist and flouring mill, which turns out for export from six to eight thousand barrels of flour per year; one sawmill, and one printing press. Water-wheels are now being put down for propelling a carding and cloth-dressing machine, and the manufacture of cloth.

"In addition, our water power, which is already sufficient for present purposes, can be

64   HISTORY OF OGLE COUNTY.

Oregon—Northern Illinois—Statistics of Ogle County—Winnebago Forum—Grand Detour Manufacturing Company.

improved to any extent, and will be another season. We know of no town where mechanics are better patronized than here, and there is still room for more, and their work is much needed."

The next number announces the death of the Rockford *Pilot* and the dying condition of the Chicago *American*.

The article on Grand Detour seems to have aroused a citizen of Oregon, for on the 28th of October appeared an article "puffing" that town. The writer gives the following business statistics of the place : "One clock and watchmaker, one saddler and harness maker, three carpenters, two cabinet makers, two painters and glaziers, one turner, one wheelwright, two masons and plasterers, two shoemakers, one blacksmith, one chair maker, three tailors, ten barbers, two stores, one grocery, two taverns, and six attorneys at law."

Nearly a month later, we find an article boasting of Northern Illinois, and setting forth its capacities and advantages. In this article is a statement that from June, 1841, to November, 1842, the settlers in this vicinity had paid at the Land office in Dixon, about $280,000—showing a rapid progress, as the settlement of this section had commenced only five or six years before.

The *Register* for December 9 gives the following statistics of Ogle county, which may be well compared with those of the present day :

"We have seventeen saw-mills, two Distilleries, one Seminary of learning, sixteen School Houses and places of public worship, ten Stores. The estimated quantity of wheat raised the present year from three hundred and

fifty to four hundred thousand bushels to say nothing of other grain, pork, beef, &c. The amount of money paid into the Land Office within the last year, by our actual settlers, is not far from $100,000.

"In addition to the River timber, which extends from one end of the county to the other, on either side of the River there are twenty-one groves, containing from one-half to six sections, or from three hundred and fifty to three thousand eight hundred and forty acres of timber each ; and so distributed over the whole as to accommodate every township in the county (which embraces twenty-one townships) at ninety-eight sections, or 62720 acres, (which we believe is too low from the information we have been able to obtain,) and distributed as it is, it places nearly every quarter section of prairie within reasonable distance of timber, which will give about one acre of timber to every six of prairie. We designed to say something of our villages, which are seven in number, but want of room prevents us this week. The rapid growth and settlement of our county is undoubtedly without a parallel in the history of the settlement of any country in the world."

The first number of the second volume is dated January 27, 1843, showing that omissions had been made during the previous year. It also purports to be "published by the Proprietors," but does not inform us who the proprietors are.

In February, we find a notice of the *Winnebago Forum*, a new Whig paper then recently started at Rockford. If our memory serves us correctly, the *Forum* was the immediate predecessor of one of the papers now published in that city.

In the latter part of March, we find an act incorporating Solon Cumins, William G. Dana and Willard A. House, and

HISTORY OF OGLE COUNTY. 65

Change of Proprietors—The Illinois Tribune—County Division—Colonizing Buffalo Grove.

their associates and successors, as the "Grand Detour Manufacturing Company," with a capital of one hundred thousand dollars.

On the 10th of May, the names of Charles H. Lamb and A. G. Henderson appear in the paper as proprietors. In July, Mr. Henderson withdrew from the concern, leaving Mr. Lamb in sole charge.

No. 26, Vol. 2, of the *Register*, dated August 25, 1843, is the last one we can find. No notice is given of its suspension, and we are at a loss to know how much longer it survived—probably, however, but a short time.

We have before us No. 7, Vol. 1, of the *Illinois Tribune*, dated at Grand Detour, December 26, 1844, and published by John W. Sweetland. As this is the only number we have been able to obtain, we can give no further intelligence concerning it. From its typographical appearance, we should suppose it to be the *Register's* successor. It contains a notice of the marriage, on the 19th of that month, by Rev. D. J. Pinckney, of Henry A. Mix to Miss Catherine J. Bennett.

In looking over the files of the *Rock River Register*, we have found a great many matters which would be of interest if republished at this time, but our limits forbid our copying them.

[NOTE.—The statement on page 51, that the county seat was *located* at Dixon, is somewhat erroneous. The first Circuit Court was held there by direction of the County Commissioners, they having the power to direct where the courts should be held. The struggle on the question of a division of the county, in 1838–9, was animated and bitter. Petitions and remonstrances were the order of the day, and much ill feeling was engendered, which has not even yet died out. As many of those taking part in the struggle are still living, we prefer to leave the matter here, without "raking up" any old feuds.]

————

CHAPTER XIV.

In 1835, George R. Webster and Stephen Hull settled in this vicinity. Several of Mr. Webster's relatives have since settled here, and the family is now quite numerous. Mr. Hull left a large number of daughters, but no sons. The daughters are nearly all married, and now living in this vicinity.

In 1835, John Waterbury and Solomon Shaver came to this section to look out a place for settlement. In the following year, they, with six other families—those of Wm. Wamsley, Wm. Nichols, B. Beardsley, Duncan Grant, Abram Schryver and Thos. Worden—numbering in all seventy-two souls, left Delaware county, N. Y., and came to Buffalo Grove, where they settled. They performed the entire journey with wagons, and were seven weeks and two days on the route, and did not sleep in a house from the time of leaving home till they reached this point. With the exception of Mr. Beardsley, now a resident of Iowa, they are all still living in the vicinity of Polo. Since their arrival, four other families of Waterburys have settled here. In point of numbers, the Waterburys, with their

7

family connections, exceed any other family in this section.

The first frame dwelling in Buffalo Grove was erected by Wm. Merritt, in 1836. This building now stands near Hon. Z. Aplington's new residence, at the north end of the town of Polo. The first frame building was a store built by John D. Stevenson, who brought the first stock of goods in this section, in 1835. In 1836, Messrs. Wales, Hunn & Co. brought another stock in here.

The first blacksmith's anvil ever used in the Rock River country is now in the possession of Hon. Z. Aplington of Polo, himself a blacksmith, to whom it was presented by the venerable John Dixon.

The settlement of the country progressed but slowly from 1837 to 1846. The land sales occurred in 1842–3, and nearly all the money in circulation was paid out for land. Men were selected to bid off whole townships for the settlers, and had anybody bid over $1.25 per acre, they would have been in imminent danger of being shot by the pioneers.

The early settlers had much difficulty with their claims. The claims were made by each one's staking out such land as he wanted—as the land was not yet in market. A claim committee was elected, regulations adopted for the government of the settlers, the clerk of the committee keeping a record of the different claims made. The Government had surveyed the land into townships, and the people subdivided it for themselves. The first committee clerk was William Illingworth, who was succeeded by Zenas Aplington. The claim committee were often

called upon to remove men who had "jumped" claims. An old settler relates an amusing story of a claim fight between V. A. Bogue and F. Cushman on one side and H. Wales and O. W. Kellogg on the other side. Bogue and Cushman had drawn a lot of rails to the "disputed territory," intending to fence the land and thereby secure its possession. Learning that this had been done, Wales and Kellogg proceeded to remove the rails, Kellogg carrying with him a "shillalah." While they were loading up, Bogue and Cushman arrived at the scene of operation. Bogue commenced throwing the rails off the wagon, while Cushman "pitched into" Kellogg and knocked him down. Wales took up the reins and started on a run with his team, Bogue following and throwing off the rails as fast as he could. Kellogg, as soon as he was knocked down, promised to leave the premises if he should be left alone. He started for his coat, which was lying on the grass near by, beside which lay his shillalah. Picking it up, he gave Cushman a sound rap over the back. Cushman then ran to a pile of rails, and by flourishing a huge rail about Kellogg, ended the fight. The quarrel about the claim was finally settled by arbitration.

At the first session of the Legislature held after Lee county was separated from Ogle, a half range of towns was taken from Carroll county and added to Ogle county on the west.

Work on the Illinois Central Railroad was commenced in this county in 1852. As the work progressed, and the prospect of its being finished became a certainty,

HISTORY OF OGLE COUNTY. 67

Illinois Central Railroad—Incorporation of Polo—Its Newspapers—Business Establishments, Churches, &c.

business in this section began to improve at a rapid rate. Zenas Aplington was the contractor for the eight miles beginning one mile south of Polo and extending seven miles north. In January, 1855, when the Railroad was completed, there were but five or six buildings in the present town of Polo. From that time to this, the town has continued to increase rapidly in population and importance.

In the month of October, 1856, the Polo *Sentinel*, the first Democratic newspaper printed in Ogle county, was commenced by F. O. Austin. It lived, however, but about three months.

In the winter of 1856–7, the Legislature passed an act incorporating the town. The first Board of Trustees consisted of J. B. More, S. E. Treat, Z. Aplington, G. R. Webster and George Swingley.

Hon. Z. Aplington, in 1854, was the owner of the principal part of the town, and he it was who gave it its present name, in honor of Marco Polo, the Venitian traveler. The name has at least one important advantage, in that there is not another town of the same name in the United States.

In June, 1857, the Polo *Transcript* was started by Chas. Meigs, Jr., who continued its publication until about the 1st of April, when the materials were purchased by the proprietor of the POLO ADVERTISER. On the 14th of April, 1858, was issued the first copy of the *Ogle County Banner*, R. P. Redfield, Publisher for a joint stock company. On the 6th of May, the first number of the ADVERTISER* was issued, since which

*See advertisement on second page of cover.

time its publication has been continued without intermission. In January, '59, Mr. Redfield purchased the *Banner* office, and at once enlarged the paper. It is a matter of no small credit to Polo that she supports her two newspapers, and supports them well.

There are now in Polo two printing-offices and newspapers, three hotels, nine grain dealers, seven dry-goods stores, two drug and book stores, two hardware stores, two millinery stores, one melodeon factory, one wind grist-mill, one steam planing mill, three blacksmith shops, two bakeries, fifteen carpenters, four shoe shops, three lawyers, two coal yards, one wagon factory, one wood turner, three tailors, one cooper shop, three harness shops, one tin shop, one paint and oil store, two painters, two dentists, four practicing physicians, one furniture room and cabinet shop, four lumber yards.

In 1857, a large and commodious Presbyterian Church was erected at a cost of about $10,000. It has a basement which is used for the purpose of a lecture room. The upper part is capable of seating five hundred persons. The building is made of brick, and is one of the first things to strike the eye in approaching the town. Rev. William E. Holyoke is the present Pastor. In June, 1858, a parish was organized under the canons of the Protestant Episcopal Church, and called Trinity Church. It is the design of the Vestry to erect a handsome and commodious church edifice during the coming summer. At present they have regular services at Union Hall. Rev. Charles J. Todd is Rector of the parish. The

Methodists have a church edifice at Buffalo Grove, and hold services on alternate Sabbaths at the school-house in Polo. Rev. S. F. Denning is their Pastor. Besides these, the Unitarians have occasional services at Union Hall. The Methodists, Episcopalians and Presbyterians maintain large and thriving Sabbath Schools.

There are large and flourishing Lodges of Odd Fellows, Good Templars and Free Masons. The first-named hold their meetings at their own Hall on Franklin street—said to be one of the finest in the State. The Good Templars and Masons hold their services in Union Hall.

Among other advantages possessed by Polo we must not fail to notice its Young Men's Association. The Association has been formed but a short time, but has already acquired a library of about one hundred volumes, to which it is making large additions. The number of members is respectable, and constantly on the increase.

There are now two free schools in operation, and the project of a graded school is being agitated with a fair prospect of success. As the town grows, educational facilities must and will keep pace with progress in other respects.

The population of Polo is now estimated at from seventeen hundred to two thousand. It is the commercial center of a large extent of territory, drawing a heavy trade from more than one-half of Carroll county on the west, and from a large share of Ogle county on the east. We know of one house alone whose cash receipts amount to over fifty thousand

dollars per annum. The business of Polo is well "backed up" by the surrounding country, an evidence of which is found in the fact that there is no station on the Illinois Central Railroad which ships a larger amount of grain in each year.

The manufactures of Polo are just in their infancy. During the year 1858, Messrs. Goodwillie, Jimmerson & Cairns erected a large steam planing mill and sash, door and blind factory, at a cost of $4,000. In the fall, F. O. Wilder commenced the manufacture of melodeons, pianos and harmoniums, and continues to increase his business at a fair rate. Messrs. Geo. Huntley & Co. are soon to commence the manufacture of R. K. Frisbee's patent broadcast sower and drill combined. There is no place in the West where a manufactory of agricultural implements will *pay* better than in Polo. An immense number of implements are sold here each year, which could be as cheaply manufactured here as elsewhere. We have no doubt our citizens would furnish a large amount of "material aid" to any such enterprise. Coal is easily obtained, timber can be procured near by, while provisions and labor can be had much more cheaply than in the large cities. A woolen factory is much needed here, and would prove a profitable enterprise to any one who might engage in it.

Building materials are plentiful and cheap. There are four stone quarries in the vicinity, from which is taken first-rate blue and gray limestone. Pine lumber comes from Chicago, and is sold in Polo at low rates.

The township organization law was adopted in this county in 1849, when the County Commissioners went out of office and the control of affairs passed into the hands of the Board of Supervisors. The last Board of Commissioners consisted of Wm. Wamsley, Willard P. Flagg and S. W. Coffman. Zenas Aplington was elected chairman of the first Board of Supervisors.

Leonard Andrus was the first white man who set his foot upon the site of the present town of Grand Detour. He traveled up the river from Dixon, in a canoe, in 1835, and made a claim at Grand Detour in the following year. In that year, Mr. Andrus and W. A. House brought their families to that place. William G. Dana, Amos Bosworth and some others arrived in 1836. The name Grand Detour signifies Great Bend. Rock River forms here, we believe, the largest bend to be found anywhere between its source and its mouth.

In 1836, the Hydraulic Company was formed for the purpose of improving the water power and erecting mills. The Company consisted of L. Andrus, A. Bosworth, W. G. Dana, W. A. House, R. Green and D. and M. Warner. They first, in 1836, built the saw-mill on Pine Creek about three miles from Grand Detour, now known as Dana's Mill. In '37, they commenced building a dam across the river at Grand Detour, and a grist and a saw-mill. These mills were not completed until February, '38. In the latter year, the Company made a division of the property and started anew. Solon Cumins, who arrived in that year,

bought one-half interest in the concern. When the mills were finished, Mr. Cumins bought the other half, and has continued to hold them until the present time. In the same year, and previous to Mr. Cumins' making the purchase, the name of the Company was changed to Rock River Mill Company. In 1835, when Andrus and House arrived at this place, they did their first cooking in the open air, with Indians standing around them.

The village of Grand Detour was laid out in 1836, when there were but a few log cabins. In '37, three frame buildings were put up—one for a store, which was occupied by a Mr. Palmer, which was also purchased by Mr. Cumins in '38; the other two were dwellings. There was also a store, started in '36, by House & Green. The settlement of the place, during the years 1837-8, progressed very rapidly. Mr. Cumins states that his purchases of goods during the years 1839-40 amounted to $40,000. His trade was very large, his customers coming from Buffalo Grove, North Grove, Cherry Grove and the whole country about.

In 1839, Messrs. Andrus & Deere commenced the manufacture of plows on a small scale. From that time to this, the business has been rapidly growing, until the Grand Detour Plow Factory has gained a wide reputation throughout the whole West. Some idea of the magnitude of their operations may be formed from the following statistics: Messrs. Andrus & Bosworth, the present proprietors, manufacture from forty to fifty plows per day—making a total of twelve thou-

74   HISTORY OF OGLE COUNTY.

Steamers on Rock River—Grand Detour as a Manufacturing Point—Settlement of Mt. Morris.

sand to fifteen thousand per annum, at a daily expense of from $150 to $175, exclusive of stock used. During the financial crisis of 1857, the factory was burned down and rebuilt in ninety days—an example of energy rarely seen save in the West. A market for their plows is found in all parts of the West, including Texas and California; and the situation of the town, on Rock River, affords excellent facilities for shipment.

The *Gipsey*, the first steamboat on Rock River, made a trip up the river in April, 1838. In 1844, the *Lighter* went up the river to Janesville. She made two or three trips, carrying freight mostly. Solon Cumins loaded her once or twice at Grand Detour, with flour. She brought goods and groceries from St. Louis.

Some seven or eight years ago, a schooner built at Kishwaukee, ran down the river and cut all the ferry ropes. The master was prosecuted at Byron, Grand Detour and Dixon, but defeated his prosecutors on the ground that Rock River was a navigable stream.

Grand Detour is admirably situated as a manufacturing point. Its water power, which has hardly begun to be developed, is one of the best in the State. Rock River affords excellent facilities for shipping manufactured fabrics to all parts of the West and Southwest; while, being only four miles from Nachusa Station, on the Dixon Air Line Railroad, shipments for the East are readily made. The steamer *Rockford* is expected to make regular trips between Dixon and Rockford during the coming season. As the country fills up, we expect to see Grand Detour growing in size and importance until it obtains even a wider reputation than at present.

At an early day, Samuel M. Hitt and Nathaniel Swingley, from Maryland, claimed large tracts of land in the vicinity of the present town of Mt. Morris. They were both men of prominence and influence, and by their representations soon induced a large number of Marylanders to settle around them. They were not without their claim difficulties, however, and prominent among their "fighting men" was one David Worden, a brawny New-Yorker, who was always on hand at any claim fight. He generally managed to remove the "jumpers" without resort to violent means; but if the latter became necessary, he was certain to carry his point. Worden is said to have been a great lover of fair play; and when any poor man in this section had had his claim jumped by an interloper, Worden made it a point of honor to remove the trespasser—peaceably if he could, but it must be done at any rate.

In the spring of 1839, Rev. L. S. Clark, ——— Boreah and John Clark, a committee appointed by the Illinois Conference of the M. E. Church, located the Rock River Seminary at Mt. Morris. The citizens of the vicinity contributed $10,000 in money and four hundred and eighty acres of land in order to secure the location of the Seminary in their midst. The contract for erecting the building was taken by J. B. McCoy, and on the 4th of July, 1839, the corner stone was laid. Dr. J. J. Beatty was Marshal of the day, and Rev. Alexander Irvine and

S. N. Sample, Esq., were the orators. At that time, there was not a single human habitation within a mile of the spot where the foundation was laid. Mr. McCoy, who was to receive eighteen thousand dollars for the job, put up a log cabin for the accommodation of his hands, and this was the first house erected in the present town of Mt. Morris. In the fall of the succeeding year, the Seminary was opened in the new building, under the superintendence of Joseph N. Waggoner, Principal, Lyman Catlin, Assistant, and Miss Cornelia N. Russell, Preceptress. Mr. Waggoner is now a bookseller and stationer in Galena. Rev. John Sharp was the first Steward of the Seminary, and the first Postmaster in the place. F. G. Petrie, Mr. Sharp's son-in-law, removed to Mt. Morris with him, and for sometime lived in a barn built by Mr. Sharp. Mr. Waggoner was succeeded as Principal by Prof. J. D. Pinckney, who held the post for a number of years.

We have before us Vol. 1, No. 20, of the Mt. Morris Gazette, dated September 20, 1850, which would make its first issue date in April of that year. It was published by J. F. Grosh and edited by Prof. D. J. Pinckney. No. 48 of the same volume, dated February 27, 1851, is the latest issue we can find under the above "administration." No. 3 of the second volume bears the names of Brayton, Baker & Co., as Publishers, and Prof. Pinckney as Editor, and is dated May 29, 1851. It says that there were no press, type, or printers in Mt. Morris, and though the paper was published there it was printed somewhere else. (We presume

at Oregon.) It speaks also of the Ogle County Gazette soon to be started at Oregon, and wishes it prosperity, &c. No. 4 is dated June 26th. It is handsomely printed, on new type, and is, typographically, the most creditable specimen of an Ogle county newspaper that we have yet seen. The Gazette only lived until about the close of the second volume, when it went down.

The Northwestern Republican was commenced in 1855, by Atwood & Williams —at least it was under the control of these gentlemen some time in that year. We believe there was a change in the firm before the paper was sold. A little more than three years ago, Myron S. Barnes purchased the concern and changed the name of the paper to Independent Watchman, which he still continues to publish.

For some years after the establishment of the institution, Rock River Seminary was rather in a languishing condition. The country was new, money was scarce, and the lack of pecuniary means materially crippled the progress of the school. Thanks, however, to the energy and perseverance of its friends, prominent among was Prof. Pinckney, it was carried through the "dark days," and is now on a solid foundation. A new and commodious building for the accommodation of the school was finished in 1856, which is full large enough for its wants for years to come. Its situation is a most desirable one. It is is on the summit of one of the highest elevations in that part of the country, and from the observatory can be seen the town of Polo and much of the surrounding country. Mt. Morris is a

72   HISTORY OF OGLE COUNTY.

Mt. Morris—Ogle County Gazette—Ogle County Agricultural Society—Oregon—Brookville—Woosung.

quiet, pleasant and healthy village, about eight miles from Polo, which is the nearest railroad station. It is entirely free from grog shops and tippling houses. The character of the school as an institution of learning is one of the best in the country. The library and apparatus, we believe, are all that could be desired. The Seminary has probably done more to educate the people of the Northwest than any other school in Northern Illinois, and we point to it with pride as one of the most valuable institutions of which Ogle county can boast.

The population of Mt. Morris is stated at from one thousand to twelve hundred. The inhabitants are principally from Vermont and Maryland.

The earliest copy we can find of an Oregon paper is No. 24, Vol. 1, of the *Ogle County Gazette*, dated November 5, 1851, and edited and published by R. C. Burchell, (now Prosecuting Attorney.) The materials used were the same employed on the first volume of the Mt. Morris *Gazette*. At the close of the first volume, Mr. Burchell changed the name of his paper to *Ogle County Reporter*, the title it still bears. For some time, the *Gazette* and *Reporter* furnished the only newspaper advertising mediums in the county, and we accordingly find advertisements from all parts of the county in their columns.

The Ogle County Agricultural Society was formed on the 4th of July, 1858. The first officers were: Thomas Stinson, President; E. P. Snow, Vice-President; James V. Gale, Treasurer; Charles W. Murtfeltt, Secretary; Henry Sharer, Clark

G. Wait, James W. Johnson, Charles O. Burroughs, John Edmonds, Managers.

In January, 1854, Mr. Burchell sold the *Reporter* establishment to Mortimer W. Smith, (now Clerk of the Circuit Court.) Mr. Smith continued its publication until July, 1857, when E. H. Leggett took charge of the paper. Mr. Leggett is still the editor and publisher.

Oregon is the county seat of Ogle county, and is situated on the west bank of Rock River, very near the geographical center of the county. It is surrounded by bluffs, making a beautiful valley for the town site. Its population is between eight and nine hundred. A substantial stone bridge is being built across the river at a cost of nearly thirty thousand dollars. The water-power here is very good, though we believe that it has been applied only to the running of a sawmill. The location of Oregon is a beautiful one, containing as handsome sites for residences as can be found anywhere in the county.

Brookville is the middle township of the western tier, lying between Buffalo and Foreston. The village of Brookville, on the extreme western edge of the town, is quite a trading point. Close at hand are Herb's saw and grist mills. From Haldane Station, in this township, a large amount of farm produce is annually shipped. There is considerable timber in the township and a plentiful supply of water.

Woosung is the most southern railroad station in the county, lying just above the line between Ogle and Lee, in Buffalo township. A town was laid out here on the completion of the railroad, by Messrs. Roundy and Brimblecom.

Lane, which, next to Polo, is the most important business point in the county, is situated in Flagg township, in the southern tier of towns, being next to the most eastern town in the tier. It is twenty-two miles from Dixon and eighty-three from Chicago, on the Dixon Air Line Railroad. Lane is one of those lively railroad towns which have sprung up, as it were, in a day. On the completion of the Air Line Road in 1855, the town was laid out, since which time it has grown at a rapid rate. Its population now numbers from twelve to fifteen hundred, and the amount of business transacted has shown a corresponding increase. The *Leader*, the first newspaper on the east side of Rock River in this county, was commenced by John R. Howlett in the fall of 1858. It meets with a good support—a fact no less creditable to the citizens of Lane than to the publisher. The country surrounding the town is well fitted for farming purposes, being the broad, rich prairie for which the entire Northern portion of Illinois is so famous. Lane is making rapid strides, and we confidently predict for her a brilliant future.

Dement, in the township of the same name, lies in the extreme southeastern corner of the county. Considerable grain and other farm produce is shipped from here each year. The village was laid out in August, 1855, by Anson Barnum and T. D. Robertson, and now contains a population of about three hundred and fifty. It is situated about half way from Chicago to the Mississippi, on the Dixon Air Line Road, and is surrounded by a rich, beautiful and productive country.

Adeline, in the township of Maryland, in the northern tier of towns, is quite an important point. It is about four miles from Foreston, on Leaf River, a small stream emptying into Rock River about six miles from Oregon. The village was laid out about the year 1846, but little more was done till about 1850, when the town started anew. Phineas Helm was the first merchant; Julius Smith, now residing at Byron, was the next. There is a good mill-privilege at the place, and a saw-mill is in operation there. Fostler's grist-mill is about a mile above the village. The population of the place is about four hundred. The country surrounding it is a high rolling prairie, well interspersed with timber, and is most excellent farming land. The settlers in the vicinity are principally from Maryland and Germany. George Mitchell, Postmaster.

The township of Foreston is the most northwestern in the county. It contains the village of Foreston, which is ten miles north of Polo and twelve miles south of Freeport, on the Illinois Central Railroad. The village was laid out in 1854 by the Vice President of the Central Railroad, Mr. Neal, who then owned the town. Soon after, John Hewitt laid out a large addition to the town, and commenced selling lots. Four years ago, as we are informed, there was not a single dwelling-house in the place. The Railroad Company built a passenger depot, freight warehouse and engine house before the road was completed. Since the completion of the railroad, the town has been growing very rapidly. A large number of dwellings, stores, warehouses, &c. were erected in the summer of 1858. The country about Foreston is the rich, high rolling prairie prevalent throughout the county. We set Foreston down as one of the most thriving and prosperous towns in the county. Samuel Mitchell, Postmaster; Matthew J. Blair, Justice of the Peace.

The population of Ogle county in 1840 was 3,479; in 1850, it was 10,020; in 1855, it was 16,456; it is now estimated at over 22,000. Churches and school-houses are plentifully distributed through the county, and twenty-four post-offices furnish mail facilities.

Ogle county is in next to the northern tier of counties. It is about evenly divided by Rock River, which runs through it from north to south. This river and its tributaries furnish some of the best water powers in the West, which have as yet hardly been touched. When this power shall be used to its full extent, Ogle will be found to be one of the best manufacturing counties in Illinois. The banks of the river in many places are surmounted with bluffs, although in some places are found beautiful, rich bottom lands. Immediately after leaving the river on either side, one comes to the broad prairie—as rich prairie, too, as the sun ever shone upon—where the soil is deep and strong, the surface undulating enough to make it picturesque and healthy, while good spring water is near at hand. The prairies in this county are thickly interspersed with luxuriant groves

of timber, thereby obviating the most plausible objection made against emigrating to the West. Everywhere, the soil is excellent, as the abundant harvests raised by our enterprising farmers can testify. Some of the largest yields ever known in the world have given the soil of Northern Illinois a name and fame abroad that is well deserved. The amount of farm products annually exported from this county is enormous, and with a ready cash market near at home, with land so fertile and cheap, it is no matter for wonder that our farmers are growing wealthy at a rate that would astonish their downcast friends. The country they inhabit is a rich and beautiful one, while the resources of the soil are not yet half developed. The counties lying between Rock River and the Mississippi are generally esteemed as being richer than any other portion of the State.

This country is as healthy as any portion of the world. Consumption, the grim destroyer so dreaded in the Eastern and Middle States, while fever and ague is almost a thing of the past; so that emigrants from the East need have no fears of this unpleasant visitor.

Men of small means, who are not compelled to "rough it" on the prairies to obtain a living, will find in Northern Illinois inducements which need only to be considered to attract them hither. Land can be bought at low rates, a ready cash market is found at any of the numerous railroad stations with which the country is interspersed, and in all these respects, the owner of a farm here is as well situated as the farmer on the main line of a railroad in New-York or Pennsylvania. The difference in yield makes an acre of prairie land equal in value to an acre of land in the Eastern States, while it can be purchased for one-half or one-third the nominal price. Settlers here find churches and schools and nearly all the comforts and luxuries of their eastern homes, at much less cost. No State in the Union affords equal facilities for the education of *the people* as Illinois; her Free School system is her greatest pride.

We have endeavored in the preceding sketches, to preserve our local records and to set forth the rapid progress of our adopted State and county. In the former, we have done the best we could, though no person can feel more keenly than we do how imperfectly the task has been performed. We have at least the satisfaction of knowing that when, in the future, some one more competent shall undertake the task, our labor will not have been in vain, and that we have done something toward collecting the materials for a HISTORY OF OGLE COUNTY.

COUNTY OFFICERS, ETC.

Representative in Congress	E. B. Washburne.
State Senator	Z. Aplington.
Representative	Joshua White.
Judge of Circuit Court	John V. Eustace.
Judge of the County Court	Virgil A. Bogue.
Clerk of Circuit Court and Recorder	Mortimer W. Smith.
Clerk of the County Court	Elbert K. Light.
State's Attorney	Robert C. Burchell.
County Treasurer	Albert Woodcock.
Sheriff	Frederick G. Petrie.
County Surveyor	Aaron Q. Allen.
School Commissioner	Dr. A. E. Hurd.
Coroner	John R. Chapman.
Master in Chancery	Joseph Sears.

POST-OFFICES AND POSTMASTERS

IN OGLE COUNTY.

Adeline	George W. Taylor.
Brookville	David Hoffhine.
Byron	George G. Swan.
Daysville	William J. Mix.
Dement	Thomas Smith.
Eagle Point	Daniel W. Fairchild.
Fitz Henry	Freeman Woodcock.
Foreston	Samuel Mitchell.
Grand Deteur	Charles Throop.
Hale	Joshua White.
Killbuck	Nathan K. Ross.
Kyte River	Alanson D. Clark.
Lindenwood	Daniel Gifford.
Lane	Jeremiah B. Barber.
Lee	George W. Northrop.
Mount Morris	Edward Davis.
Ogle	Aaron Weeks.
Oregon	Edmund P. Sexton.
Payne's Point	Willard P. Bump.
Polo	George D. Read.
Taylor	Dexter Stocking.
Wales	Thomas Hillar.
White Rock	George Ambrose.
Woosung	William Brimbleoom.